Happiness 24x7

OM PRAKASH NEMANI

Become
Shakespeare
.com

First published in 2018 by

Becomeshakespeare.com
Wordit Content Design & Editing Services Pvt Ltd
Unit - 26, Building A-1, Nr Wadala RTO, Wadala (East),
Mumbai 400037, India
T:+91 8080226699

This book has been funded by WORDIT ART FUND
WORDIT ART FUND helps deserving
Authors publish their work
To apply for funding, please visit us at
becomeshakespeare.com

©
ISBN: 978-93-87649-15-6

Disclaimer:
This is a work of fiction. Names, characters, business,
place, event and incidents are either the product of the
author's imagination or used in a fictitious manner. Any
resemblance to actual person, living or dead or actual
event is purely coincidental.

Contents

Foreword

Sadguru Ramesh Ji
Poorna Ananda Ashram
Hyderabad

Life could be lived in two ways.
One LIFE LIVES YOU and Two YOU LIVE LIFE.

When life lives you, you get influenced and affected by every situation of life. You feel happy when something is favourable and you get depressed when things are unfavourable. But when you live life, you have full control over your emotions; you don't get affected by situations. You are always unconditionally peaceful and happy irrespective of life situations.

As Human Beings we have the option to choose one among these two ways of life and we have the potential too to live that life.

Nemaniji, in this book has raised a beautiful question as to what is it that we want most in life? We may have money, power, fame, success but still our background, personalities, aspirations and goal might seem very different - we all want to be happy. Happiness is not an abstract concept. It is a state of mind, a condition of life which is our birth right as human beings.

Nemaniji, after experiencing all sorts of adventures in life is born with the ideas and ways to lead a happier life. The reader of this book will feel the excitement of search and discovery and will find that following the path to happiness is so easy.

The whole book is completely focused, so as to empower people to take charge of their lives and awaken their pure inner selves. The book emphasises on adopting simple ways of spirituality to keep oneself happy 24x7. Spirituality is not about doing things or becoming someone, it is just about being who we truly are. The thoughts reverberates through this book are incidents, interactions and own experiences of Nemaniji. This book has kept in its center point the situation that brings you to the fore; the external human conflicts that have held us in thrall since the beginning of life. Since, every chapter of the book you are holding at this moment is so closely connected to our lives that it will have an empowering effect on you. It may ignite in you the confidence to take charge of your life and awaken to your pure and perfect inner self. It will enable you to begin to unravel your own subconscious beliefs and perceptions that control your thoughts, feelings and actions.

This book will encourage you to make a beginning of Self-transformation and to take first step towards happiness. The moment you start the journey of transformation you will become a SAINT and will be able to create a life of joy, Contentment and bliss.

Happiness is a decision; we have to take it with determination and commitment, taking full responsibility of its result. The book has highlighted that the goal of knowledge is to transform the mind from its limited understanding to a more expanded state of awareness.

Sadguru Rameshji
Poorna Ananda Ashram
Janwada Hyderabad India

ABOUT THE AUTHOR

Om Prakash Nemani, born on 5th September 1936, in Kanpur is a graduate in commerce. He did his early schooling in Kanpur and graduated from Lucknow University. He was awarded Gold Medal and Chancellor's Medal by Shri V.V. Giri. Former President of India. He started his career as a Probationary officer in State Bank of India. Since, he belongs to a business family he left the job after five years of service and started his own manufacturing unit. He is widely travelled and has vast experience of various fields of business.

Since last 3 years he has come in touch with Sadhguru Rameshji and is moving ahead on his journey on the path of spirituality. Nemani considers him a common man just like you living with family, earning his livelihood and moving in a society with very strong belief systems of happiness through materialistic success. He is keen and eager to explore and unlock the secrets of constant happiness and as such his writing consists of so many random ideas to be in constant happiness 24/7 by blending simple spirituality, living in the family and a society which has very fixed and settled norms of achieving happiness.

He can be reached via his face book page or via email at ompnem@gmail.com. Book can be ordered on Amazon.

ACKNOWLEDGEMENT

My quest for writing a book on being Happy blended with Spirituality goes back to my Sanskars given by my mother, but the seed of the idea was lying dormant till 2016, when I first met Sadhguru Ramesh Ji of Poorna Ananda Ashram Hyderabad in a spiritual retreat at Rishikesh.

After meeting him I realised that even remaining in family, doing business and actively participating in all activities social, Politics and religious in the society one can practice spiritualism in life. In our everyday behavior we can be benefitted by practicing and adopting small things of spirituality. We can be a better human being, better entrepreneur and better CEO of our business. We can perform more efficiently and humanely in our profession and service and overall remain healthy and happy.

I have been listening lots of Pravchans and various Kathas with my wife. She was my conscience keeper. Since, she expired in 2006, I was having vacuum Sadhguru Ramesh Ji filled that vacuum and inspired me to proceed on this path of spirituality. My friend, spiritually enlightened, Zen Meditation Practitioner Aditya Ajmera Ji of Mumbai also guided me and inspired me for my venture. I am especially thankful to Shri Aditya Ji for giving his inputs on every step. He has also contributed many of his wisdom full thoughts and quotes in my every chapter.

I have benefited myself with this venture, as during this process I listened Sadhguru Jaggi Vasudeva, Brahma Kumari, Sister B.K.Shivani, Swami Sukhabodhanand Ji, Sadhguru Ramesh Ji and have learnt many things. Since I decided to write book I have listened them with a view to adopt them in life and experience.

I could never imagine, what was looking impossible and impractical now looking quite possible, doable and adoptable. I am also very much thankful to my sons Arun Nemani, Ajay Nemani, my daughter in law Archana Nemani and entire family who extended their full support and encouraged me all the times. I acknowledge the cooperation extended to me by the entire team of our organisation specially Mr.LijoLona, Mr.G. Venkateswarulu Ms. Sushma Rasaily, Mr.Manjunath HS and Mr.Ankit Singh.

I am extremely grateful to my publisher, the creative team at Wordit Content Design and Editing Services, a sister concern of leadstart Publishing, for funding my project by Wordit Art Fund and for getting it published under their brand Become Shakespeare.com.

INTRODUCTION

Excerpts from books by Paramahansa Yogananda

"It is not possible to attain happiness without non-attachment"

"You don't need to seek understanding outside yourself - everything you want to know exists within yourself"

"Darkness cannot exist where there is light"

"Many people use their powers of reasoning cleverly to justify their delusions"

"If you want to be sad, no one in the world can make you happy. But if you make up your mind to be happy, no one and nothing on earth can take that happiness from you"

"You are a master when you can use your senses, but they don't use you"

"Life has a bright side and a dark side, for the world of relativity is composed of light and shadows. If you permit your thoughts to dwell on evil, you yourself will become ugly. Look only for the good in everything so you absorb the quality of beauty"

"In the spiritual life one becomes just like a little child - without resentment, without attachment, full of life and joy"

"Real happiness can stand the challenge of all outer experiences. When you can bear the crucifixions of others' wrongs against you and still return love and forgiveness; and when you can keep that divine inner peace intact despite all painful thrusts of outer circumstance, then you shall know this happiness."

****

We are all blessed souls. The almighty has given us this beautiful human body as part of his being. The nature has provided us everything required to remain alive and happy. I was born on 5th September 1936 and had an inclination to become a teacher. I could not become a teacher and still find myself a student always trying to learn and be inquisitive about the human behaviour. During my this journey of life I have experienced and seen very closely that people are having everything and still their mind is creating all sorts of obstacles in their way to remain happy and joyful all the time. This human life is very precious and has been given counted moments to remain happy and joyful all the time. Any moment we are unhappy, sad or having any negative feelings and thoughts; we are actually wasting our precious moments which we cannot get back.

I am one of you living with family performing all day to day, social, financial and personal obligations. I am also part of the same society which is driven by certain traditions and belief systems. I have also found it hard to come out of those established traditions and belief systems. We create comfort zone and find it easy to live within those established norms and conditioning of the society.

In this book, I have tried to address my concern that how because of our ignorance and unawareness we are wasting our precious moments and purpose of our life. We have the strength and power to avoid these sorrows and pain which we are inflicting on ourselves. I feel just by adopting small changes or techniques and getting aware at such moments, we can avoid those emotions to generate in our mind which are causing these pains and sorrows; are weakening our strength and are forcing us to waste our precious moments of life.

We are very powerful and energetic soul. As we know sunlight is full of energy and we can see it with naked eye but if we focus that light through magnifying glass, it becomes so powerful that it can create an enormous heat. Similarly, soul energy, when focused through our purpose of BEING, will become power which will reflect in our behaviour and interaction. The magnifying glass is our purpose.

Goals in our life are the milestones in our journey of life. They are what we want to achieve in our doings. Purpose of life is how we are BEING, the qualities we are experiencing and radiating while we are working towards our goals.

We read and listen, lots of discourses and attend sermons etc. We do lot of SATSANG. All are full of Gyan or Knowledge. All are good for our soul. They all give us information, now we have to put them in practice to alter our life. The purpose of this book is to transform the information and make it so easy that you start practicing them and then be like that. When the information is put into practice it becomes experience and when we become like that it becomes wisdom. Main purpose of this book is to give information, convert it into your personal experience and then let it become your wisdom.

Spirituality makes mind silent. We all know, we can create best thoughts, can take best decisions; can feel pleasure from within only when our mind is silent, not having any noise. Meditation makes mind silent.

I have been listening lots of Discourses and Sermons. Since, 1985 I am going to these Satsangs and Kathas and have been trying to move on the path of religion and spirituality. In this period I attended many Kathas of most respected Dongare Ji Maharaj, Respected Ramesh Bhai Ojha, Respected Morari Bapu, and respected Kirit Bhai and of others. But as per tradition of the family, my focus, while attending these Kathas was more religious than spiritual. These all Satsangs and Kathas were very good and helped me immensely to achieve contentment to a great extent. These traditional religious events helped me to remain quite stable in the times of difficulties.

"I will like to share with you one of my personal experience. In 1980s I was having acute family problem and I was very tense. One day one of my cousins just asked me to listen to BHAGWAT KATHA of Respected Dongare ji Maharaj. I had just decided to go for one day but it impressed me so much that I continued to listen it for another eight days till it was over. It gave me so much peace of mind and contentment that from that time I became absolutely calm and stable. I was not having any stress and was just watching it as it was happening".

Since, recently in the last three years, I have come in touch with spiritual Sadhguru Sri Ramesh Ji of Poorna Ananda Ashram, Hyderabad and Zen Meditation Practitioner Aditya Ajmeraji, from Mumbai I have developed interest to learn and practice spirituality in practical life. This developed lot of inquisitiveness to know more and more about spirituality. I developed interest to listen Sadhguru Jaggi Vasudev, Brahma Kumari Sister B. K.Shivani, Sadhguru Ramesh Ji and Swamy Sukhabodhananda etc. I also got the opportunity of listening them in various programs and spiritual retreats etc. The thoughts expressed in this book are the result of all those listening and readings.

This spiritual treasure derived by me through these teachers helped me to come out of the comfort zone and break some of the belief systems. It has enabled me to some extent to develop a confidence, that I cannot just only control my various emotions like anger, getting hurt, feeling insulted, getting tempted, feeling jealous and develop hatred for some, but can tune my mind to take my permission before creating these emotions.

With my personal experience, I am trying to share through this book with readers some small techniques, which will help you to come out of the self created comfort zone and make you spiritually enlightened and achieve constant happiness 24/7. This initially looks difficult but once one starts practicing them, it becomes routine rituals/way of living, If somebody is shouting, it is not necessary that we will have to shout. Simply we have to just talk to him patiently and see that he also will stop shouting.

We somehow develop belief system that in all Discourses and Sermons we get the same things, all teach the same things; people say and preach lot of things but we always feel whether they are following them; whatever they say is just for saying; it is not practical; they have not experienced the hardships of the life which we are facing; time has changed; their times were different now these things don't hold any ground, ultimately we justify ourselves that whatever, we are doing is correct and we just listen and read but still remain the same.

A Zen Master when explaining stress management to an audience raised a glass of water and asked:

"How heavy is this glass of water?" Answers called out ranged from 20g to 500g. The master replied, "The absolute weight doesn't matter. It depends on how long you try to hold it. If I hold it for a minute, that's not a problem. If I hold it for an hour, I'll have an ache in my right arm and neck. If I hold it for a day, you'll probably have to call an ambulance. In each case, it's the same little weight, but the longer I hold it, the heavier it becomes."

He continued, "And that's the way it is with our life. If we continue to carry our burdens all the time, sooner or later, the burden becomes increasingly heavy and we won't be able to bear it" Better we learn to drop our burden regularly to maintain our well-being"

There is a very simple suggestion for such people that they should analyze themselves and find out one such of their Sanskars or habit, about which they feel that it is not good and many a times it is disturbing their happiness and peace. Then they should listen or read some of the Discourse of any of the Guru, in which they have even slightest belief. They should concentrate on their only one aspect, which they have pinpointed. Supposing they select one thing because of which they get disturbed or excited quickly on small incidents, then they should work on that as per the saying of the Guru which they have selected. Now you will see the miracle in a very short span of time beyond your imagination.

SAINT is one who is aware of his BEING, a pure soul, who always tries to clean his soul. A person who is remembering and is aware all the time that he is a pure soul is a SAINT. Even after knowing this because of SANSKARS, his soul is getting dust of anger, hurt, jealousy, ego, cheating and other things. If he tries to clean it and comes back to his originality, he is a SANT, may not be living in ASHRAM. SATSANG is living with people, who have started the process of cleaning their soul. We can experience it by coming together for some 30-45 minutes, spending time together, trying to clean our anger, hurt, greed, jealousy etc and coming out clean.

It has been proved scientifically through various researches carried out by many Universities including Harvard University that brain and body can not differentiate between real and imagination. We ourselves feel that in the sleep when we see a dream, it looks real to us. It is so because real and imagination is the same for the soul. We should make it a practice to see ourselves every day in the morning and night before sleep. We have to see and visualize of a place, which is in our recent memory and where we get peace and positive vibrations, we will find ourselves in that place. Visualization is a power, which is increased by practice.

Past is impression, Future is expectation and Present is realization. We should constantly try to delete the past impressions and don't get attached to future expectations. This will keep us in present all the time

Spirituality is not only for salvation but it makes you best CEO (Chief Executive Officer) of your own self. Spiritualism teaches you, how you can bring best out of you. It tells we have all the qualities required to be happy in life constantly 24/7. We have the power to separate our mind from body. We always experience that our mind is not always there where we are sitting. It flows away from our body to somewhere else, where it is more interested. We also have the power to get angry with some people and don't get angry with another set of people. At times we control our anger, don't react and respond and on another occasion with other people we get angry very soon and start shouting. It all shows that we have the power to control our emotions and make the mind work as we wish. So we have the power to control our mind and emotions, but we don't exercise our power because we are not aware of it. Spiritualism makes you aware of it and takes one step ahead when it gives you strength to think that you simply don't just have power to control, but you have power beyond that. Gradually by practice, you can make your mind attuned to your instructions. The mind will not be able to create any thoughts without your permission. We behave differently with different people in a similar situation. It shows that our mind obeys us and when we give it permission to be angry with someone it starts shouting and when we don't give it permission to be angry with someone, it remains silent.

Spirituality develops the inner qualities which make human perfect and above normal being. We are proud that India with the blend of spiritualism has given CEOs to head top 10 Global Tech Companies. There are more Indian origin CEOS than any other nationality after Americans in most fortune 500 companies of the world. Times Magazine termed CEOS as India's leading export and said that the sub-continent could be the ideal training ground for global bosses.

Spirituality teaches us timeless wisdom i.e. wisdom which is beyond time, place and circumstance; which is true all the time. Spirituality emphasizes on knowledge, principles, values, integrity, character, morality and guidance.

Always remember God has sent us to be happy only. We have limited indefinite time with us, so enjoy every moment. Best way to make God happy; be happy all the time. Best Puja, Worship or Gift to God is JOY and JOY. Be, JOYFUL-GOD will be HAPPY.

We can explain the whole contents of the book in the following quote of a learned philosopher

Quote from William Henry Channing

"To live content with small means; to seek elegance rather than luxury, and refinement rather than fashion, to be worthy, not respectable, and wealthy, not rich; to study hard, think quietly, talk gently, act frankly, to listen to stars and birds, to babes and sages, with open heart, to bear all cheerfully, to all bravely await occasions, hurry never. In a word, to let the spiritual unbidden and unconscious grow up through the common. This is to be my symphony."

GRATITUDE

Quote from Sri Sri Ravi Sankar

"Welcome each day with a genuine SMILE from within. That Smile comes when you know for Sure that DIVINE LOVES YOU".

Quote from Sadhguru Jaggi Vasudev

"What is possible and what is not is not your business. Nature will decide this. Your business is just to work for what truly matters to you. The divine is constantly waiting at your doorsteps to move in if only you allow the necessary space".

Every morning when you wake up think you are alive and see around you for the people who matters to you are also alive. Give a big smile that you are alive; Give another big smile that everybody around you who matters is also alive. Every day more than one million people don't wake up and more than 10 million people lose every morning someone who matters to them in life. So give a big smile and thanks to the nature/ supreme power. This will remind you every morning how precious is your life. We are all mortal beings and have counted fixed moments. We have to be aware every moment that it is very precious and we cannot waste it. Everything else is there for us only if we are alive. Every moment passed cannot be retrieved. We have no means to earn it back.

A grateful mind never takes things for granted. As you express your gratitude, you must not forget that the highest appreciation is not to simply utter words, but to live by them daily. Gratitude includes giving back. The highest tribute to the people and circumstances you have lost is not grief but gratitude. Be thankful that your paths crossed and that you got the chance to experience something wonderful.

To be truly grateful you must be truly present. We often forget that the greatest miracle is not to walk on water; the greatest miracle is to walk on this green earth, dwelling deeply in the present moment, appreciating it and feeling completely alive. Letting go of control multiplies the potential for gratitude. Learn to let go, relax a bit and ride the path that life takes you sometimes. Try something new, be fearless but above all else, do your best and be OK with it. Clearing yourself of needless expectations lets you truly experience the unexpected. And the greatest joys in life are often the unexpected surprises and opportunities you never anticipated.

"Life should be lived with a little more gratitude and a little less attitude". Let's consider how fortunate we are – let's consider it every day. The more we count our blessings, the more blessings there will be to count. The more you are in a state of gratitude the more you will attract things to be grateful for. Being happy won't always make you grateful, but being grateful will always make you happy. Gratitude fosters true forgiveness, which is when you can sincerely say, Thank you for that experience.

Anything when stuck in the tooth, tongue keeps going on that spot. Tongue can also go to the other teeth where nothing is stuck, but the tongue has a nature. Similarly mind has also the nature to stick where we have problem; it does not go to the moments where we have no problems. We should focus on the good which is happening and deal with the problems where they are happening in our lives. Let us not consume our minds on negativity; let us consume our minds on positivity. Focus on the positive and deal with the negative. Gratitude is the attitude which gives us the fortitude to deal with the toughest challenge in the life.

You never need more than you have at any given moment. Gratitude is all inclusive. Good days give you happiness and bad days give you wisdom. This is especially true to your relationships what you have to be grateful for in the present changes. Be grateful for all you have now, because you honestly never know what will happen next.

Human race is evolving every moment. We have come to the present age evolving from forest age. God has given brain and intellect to human being and with the help of that lots of innovations and inventions have been made by the human being. This is a continuous process and human being is evolving every day. Technology and researches in all the fields have made the life of human being more comfortable and innovative. This all technological changes and education has developed a sense of pride and ego in human race.

We have to analyze that what are the things which we got because of our ignorance and what things we got through our efforts with the help of worldly information. If we think right from our birth we will have to introspect; how we got birth; how we came on this earth as a human being; how we got good parents; how we got a good family; how we got good people on every step; how we got help and cooperation in our difficult days; how we are getting air, sunlight, water, etc so essential for our living alive; we will understand that all these things we got through our ignorance without making any effort.

We have started thinking ourselves so wise that we have developed a belief system that we can do anything and we are capable of taking care of ourselves without any help of any unknown factor. As a matter of fact this belief system that we have acquired everything and we can do everything and anything is the biggest ignorance.

We also understand that from where we got these Sanskars of love, happiness and purity. Right from our birth we started enjoying and loving anybody whosoever was coming in contact with love and smile. How we learnt to smile back to anybody and everybody without discriminating about any cast, creed or color, rich or poor.

Many a times, when we earn some name, fame and wealth, we get under illusion that this all we have achieved through our intellect and hard work. If we go deep into it, we will find that this all has also happened only because somebody inspired us to accept somebody's advice and gave us strength to act upon that. Somebody gave us proper understanding and strength at the right time and right moment. We know it very well that it is not permanent and we can lose it at any time. But we live in illusion that we have earned it through our intellect and hard work and we remaining the same person, can never lose it.

We have to understand that even our intellect and capacity to work hard is also not permanent. We are vulnerable to commit mistake and lose our capacity to work hard. We all know that there is some power which is playing vital role in making us what we are today. Even after knowing this we do not accept it, because in accepting that we feel defeated. It is not difficult to accept defeat from person mightier than us, but it is very difficult to accept somebody as mightier than us. It requires a huge effort to accept somebody else as mightier than us. Our ego comes in the way of acceptance.

We have been listening lots of Sermons and Discourses and we all know the secret of happiness is in remaining in present only; remaining detached; always take care of your parents, love everybody; speak truth; always accept good qualities of others and adopt good advices. These things do have effect on us; we think of adopting them also because we find them near to our heart. But the dust which has come on our originality from times immemorial we are not able to move towards adopting them. It is because we have developed a belief system that they are difficult to adopt and they are meant for just listening and very difficult to follow and adopt.

It all is happening because we trust our intellect and hard work more and forget our awareness. We have to be aware all the time that we have got much more and all the necessary things to live without our efforts and we have to be grateful to that power which has provided us that all. We have to practice every day. We should also understand that where love, truth, peace and happiness is in built within ourselves, nature has also installed certain emotions in us as Anger, Jealousy, Greed, Ego, Guilt etc to keep us always in illusion. We have to win over them. We can make them our friend rather than enemy. We have to practice every day that they will act only with our permission. Only listening will not do any good to us, we will have to practice them every day.

People are often unreasonable, self centered; forgive them. If you are honest, people may cheat you; but remain honest; what you are doing to build, people may destroy overnight, but continue building. It is between you and God. It never goes between you and the people.

My mother used to say always, whenever, we were leaving home; TAKE GOD ALONG WITH YOU. She used to say always with a pat on our shoulders very mildly and sincerely with all her love; take God along with you and your work will be done. If we wish to be happy learn to walk with God today and trust Him for the morrow. This was giving us so big strength that we were all the time having a feeling, and even today we have the feeling that God is moving with us and we have no problem as we have the support of the almighty.

So I have to urge you all; pay your gratitude to the God every morning and always carry a feeling that he is always with you. It will remove all your fear and pain and will strengthen you and your soul. This very thought will keep you away from Ego and you will never worry from the difficulties. You will always have self confidence and will feel that the whole world is there just to help you. You will never generate negative thoughts. Your mind will always take your permission to respond to any situation. You will stop reacting to any situation, circumstance or to person and you will always respond with full responsibility because your mind will take your permission before responding.

In our lifetime we many a times face success and failure, which may change the pattern of our life. Success and failure both are the two sides of a coin. But in a Toss if you don't get your call right it is failure. Just think, how much experienced you may be, you just can't call right all the time. Sometimes you may call correctly and sometime your call may not come correct. When our call is correct we call it success and when our call is wrong we call it failure.

As a matter of fact we can call but we cannot control whether our call will be right or wrong. Similarly, we can do our job but we cannot predict or control its result. Success makes us happy and failure disappoints us. Let us just think that both had just happened, as we have no control on them. It will make you stable and strengthen you to face both the situations with cool and stable mind.

This feeling of stability, if we take as God's will, we will neither be over excited nor over disappointed. Sometimes we feel that it is necessary to get very intensely involved to get good result. It is true we should put all our efforts; give 100%, whatever we do but we should feel happy about our efforts; we should not make our happiness dependent upon the result.

We should pay gratitude to our soul consciousness, which is making us so powerful that we can remain stable and calm equally in success and failure. This mental strength comes from the pure soul consciousness. It saves us from adopting any unfair or wrong means to achieve success. Because the moment we think of adopting any means whatsoever to achieve success, we deplete our soul consciousness and we get attached to the result of the pursuit and lose focus.

Best way to pay gratitude is meditation every day. Meditation means focusing on certain thought thinking of no other thought. One may do it by adopting certain mantra or thought or viewing his breathing or certain point in the body. This can be done once or throughout the day. This slows down creation of thoughts and leaves little space for negative thoughts. It stops depletion of energy so it preserves energy. Ultimately, it is like saving meaning earning and spending thoughtfully.

Living a meaningful and worthy life demands a redirection of our attitude and actions.

LOVE YOURSELF

Quote from Swami Sukhabodhananda

"Just be a witness and do not get identified. Relax your body, your mind and then finally just be a witness. Let not your 'I' get identified with your body and mind. This dis-identification is meditation".

Make you your best friend. Be aware, you, can be your worst enemy also. Take care of yourself and Love yourself. When others criticize us, we can reject their opinion and protect ourselves, but when we criticize us the mind accepts the criticism. We cannot protect ourselves from self criticism. When the mind creates critical thoughts about the self, do not suppress or avoid it. Address every thought and gently change it with understanding and shift from self criticism to self motivation. When we make a mistake and criticize ourselves and reaffirm that we are weak, we are giving ourselves the permission to repeat the mistake. Self criticism depletes soul power. We need this power so that we do not repeat our mistakes. Irrespective of all of our mistakes, we need to remind ourselves- "I am a powerful soul and I can do it right this time". Shift the mind from self pity/Self-criticism to self-awareness and self-evaluation.

Since, we know, it is always better to appreciate we normally appreciate others. We should also learn to appreciate ourselves. When we criticize ourselves and start hating us we will radiate negative energy to us. You are coming in interaction with others less than you are interacting with you. So we will make strong impact what we are saying to us. When we will be negative with us we will radiate the same to others. If you are low and depressed but you want to appreciate others and send positive emotions to others, you may utter good words but your inner negative vibrations will radiate and your words will have no impact.

Lao tsu*: "He who knows others is wise. He who knows himself is enlightened."*

What we will create inside we will experience the same. Everybody around you may be having love for you but if you do not love yourself you will not be able to experience other's love. If you are wearing lots of warm clothes you will not feel cool in an air conditioned room. So when you are not having love for yourself then you will not believe, others are having love for you. You will find their love artificial.

We should never compare ourselves with someone. Sometimes we feel that we are trying to reduce our wants as it is good for us, but get tempted by seeing others, who are increasing their wants and see we can afford but still we are depriving ourselves of the things. Initially it may create pressure, but the moment we start enjoying our act of reducing our wants we will get rid of pressure and leave comparing ourselves with others. We have to create beautiful relationship with ourselves to have good relationship with others. Relationship with us should be good and powerful.

Our journey of self transformation has to be checked in reference only to ourselves, no comparison with others. Appreciate yourself for the smallest change made. Be careful when you talk to yourself because you are listening.

The body is tree while soul and thinking is seed. We have not to work on tree, but we have to work on seed. The soul is the seed; the energy that it creates has an effect on our emotional health, physical health and relationships.

We think we can control our mind, but we have to be powerful to overpower our mind. When we want to control, we try to control by blaming others for not being able to control. We have to make ourselves powerful to see that we do not create the thoughts, which we do not want. Instead we control them when they come. Control give rise to blame and taking responsibility leads to improve. Whatever, thoughts we are creating we are responsible. Taking responsibility will make us conscious to create any thought and when we will create some thought consciously we will like to act on it and will always find it useful for us.

Jallaudin Rumi: *"Your task is not to seek for love, but merely to seek and find all the barriers within yourself that you have built against it"*

Complaining depletes our energy because we are thinking about that which is not in our control. Complaining means focusing on the problem and concern is focusing on the solution.

One may agree to disagree with someone for avoiding further discussion or arguments, but never agree to disagree with your consciousness. We are having a constant discussion between our mind and consciousness. Our mind always forces us to agree to disagree with our consciousness. Many a times, we have experienced that whenever we agree to mind to disagree with our consciousness we are trapped and later we have to regret for that decision. So we should develop a Sanskar that we will never agree to disagree with our consciousness. If we want to give light to others we have to glow ourselves. What we think we become. Your respect for you is your biggest asset. Changing *or* altering of habits is a journey. It will take some time but it will not take lives. We can change if we are aware, attentive and conscious of our behaviour inside the house, our own room.

We are different outside, why because we have allowed ourselves to behave differently. Our programming is done by ourselves. Fear should not be motivation understanding should be motivation, I want health, I want peace and I want happiness. Worldly success creates happiness when things happen, as per your wish. But if you want to create permanent happiness you will have to create happiness inside, irrespective of the situations. We have the power to agree to disagree. We are doing it every day. We agree to mind to disagree with our inner consciousness. We have simply to reverse it. We should agree to disagree with our mind, when our inner conscious does not want to agree with the mind. First we lose control on our mind then words and then action. We cannot call it natural and accept it. We have moved so much from natural that we are now learning, how to laugh. We are searching reasons to make us laugh.

When we start moving towards spirituality it also creates some pressure. But we should take it as we start anything say walking for good health, we will have some pressure of walking in the initial days. But this pressure is good for good health. Similarly when we think of the health of our mind and habits we may create some pressure but gradually we will see that pressure will become pleasure.

Blaming, complaining and criticizing discharges the soul battery and we feel mentally exhausted. Instead of blaming situations for our fatigue let us take personal responsibility of the emotions we create. Like we take care of our words and behaviour with others let us take the same care in our conversation with ourselves. While watching the television news, sports or any scene; practice creating an emotion different from the emotion of the screen. This is taking charge of our mind.

When we create the energy of peace and love in a situation only then we will be able to experience it. The more we create negative emotions in a situation the lesser we experience our original positivity and then we start looking for peace, love and happiness outside.

Nisargdatta Maharaj: *"Real Love never judges, it does not condemn others, criticize or it's punitive. It unites, welcomes, protects and nurtures the growth of humanity".*

If we think, what we have always done, as right, then we will get what we have always got. To change our Sanskars we need knowledge and power. Only listening and reading good words is not enough to create a change. The soul is mind, intellect is sanskars. Mind creates thought, intellect takes a decision, but when it repeatedly comes into action it will become a Sanskar. We were doing things so that we could experience peace, happiness and all the qualities of the being. We thought doing will make us experience the being truth, but we will experience the being only when we express it in the doing.

When we energies to others, we are the first one to experience it. We get what we give to others. When we think or speak negatively to another person the extent to which they get affected is their choice. But we will not be able to stop the negative energy from affecting our own mind and body. If we copy the unpleasant behaviour of others we block our beautiful qualities. Let us radiate our qualities in interaction with them. Each soul has been on a long journey, creating different Sanskars in each birth. Two souls cannot have the same Sanskars. Let us not expect people to have same qualities as us.

When we do something for someone, let us not feel that we are doing it for them. If we have negative thoughts of unwillingness neither we nor they will be happy. We are doing it because of this relationship and their happiness is important to us. Sometimes people may not behave the way we want, let us consciously shift our mind to their past pleasant behaviour. This enables us to see them in a positive perspective and then respond to the present situation in the right manner.

One level of giving is if we expect something maybe appreciation, name or fame. One step further, if we feel that somebody requires something and if we are giving, we think that it is good for us to give but the highest level of giving is we just give without thinking of anything that is selfless giving. When we shift from expecting respect to giving love and respect we shift from the taking mode to giving mode. While giving we feel light and happy because we are the first to experience the energy of love.

We believe that it is survival of the fittest. Purpose of our life is not to survive only, it is to serve. Everything in nature is for serving others. Our purpose is to serve others with our vibrations of love and peace. In the survival mode we create competition, fear and anger. In the service mode we create co-operation, sharing and caring making us emotionally strong.

The intention behind the Karma should be pure and selfless. When we do charity, let there not be any thought of getting recognition or validation in return. When the karma is selfless, the energy flows from inside out because we do not expect anything in return. The energy of giving flows through and empowers us.

Let us go to work with the intention of giving and sharing our knowledge, talents, skill and giving co-operation appreciation and responsibility. Based on our wisdom and experience we should give our opinion to people. Even if they reject it our role is to give. Don't expect that it will always be implemented. Let us create an attitude of Gratitude towards everyone we meet and everything we use.

We should make our mind tuned to think positive thought for everybody. So the best we can give to anybody are our positive vibrations. Our thoughts and feelings create our energy field. The energy field has an effect on our body, on people, on nature and on matter; our consciousness vibrates into universe. If our energy field is pure and powerful everyone will get touched with our pure vibrations. This will help them to emerge their own purity and power. This is the true meaning of blessing people.

The food we eat has an effect on our mind. Non Vegetarian food has vibrations of hatred, fear, anger and hurt because in the process it had caused the same emotions in some other living being. When we consume non-vegetarian food, we also consume these vibrations and they have an effect on our mind and body.

The wisdom we get from our elders is on the basis of what is right for us according to our culture and environment. Science tells us what is right for our body. Spirituality tells us what is right for our soul.

There is a difference between criticism and giving critical energy. For pointing out any body for his mistake or for his inefficiency we have to point out the mistake or inefficiency but not the person. If we criticize the person we are sending negative vibrations and it will create negativity in him also and will bounce back to the person who is criticizing. So while giving feedback we have to separate the person from the act and we have to talk for correcting the act and not person. We have to give feedback not criticize him and that too with love.

Giving feedback and opinion is different from criticism. Feedback talks about the deed; criticism attacks the doer. When someone makes a mistake we can explain them their mistake and focus on how they can do it better the next time. Criticism attacks how they have done it wrong in the past

We have programming from childhood that we are good only if people appreciate us. We wear clothes only keeping in mind that what others will like. We don't care how much love we are having for others. Because we feel it is not visible and what we wear is visible to others. We should not harm anybody but we should do what gives happiness to us and our family. When we become dependent on people's approval for taking our decisions in life then we may take decisions which are not comfortable for us. Different souls because of different past and present Sanskars will always have different opinions in the same situation. It is not possible to get everyone's approval for any choice we make. If needed take advice and opinions from family and friends before taking a decision. But do not make choices to please people and get their appreciation.

The original qualities of the soul radiate when it is calm and stable. When we keep getting affected by other's opinion we will remain disturbed and this blocks our energy of love. Sometimes, we unintentionally compete and think that nobody will be able to do what I can do. We have to be aware that we should feel good if others do better than us and feel as good as we feel when we perform well. It will create energy field with love. We many a times compete even with our children, spouse and even more near and dears. It is a natural process but if we are aware we will not feel likewise and create more love.

Comparison and competition comes from the feeling of being and doing better than others. When we feel that we are better than others it increases our self worth. Feelings of competition created in professional life become our Sanskar. Our Sanskar makes us compete with family and friends and blocks our energy of love.

When others in family are able to do something better than us or have better relationships we should appreciate their qualities. If we create jealousy or feel inferior we are sending them negative energy. Our intention should be to be and do the best of our capacity. Focus on our qualities and skills and keep doing better in reference to our own qualities and capacity not in reference to other people. Purpose of life is to be our best not better than others. Wanting to be better than others is a never ending race. We will not be happy because there will always be someone ahead of us. Fear, stress, anger, insecurity and jealousy will be created with feelings of competition.

We all come with Synch destiny with each others. Many a times we feel we are doing lots for others but are not getting the response to that effect. If we feel good if we help somebody and we enjoy then we should not expect the response because we are doing it for our happiness. We should be aware that if we are enjoying harming anybody then we will definitely get back the same in some way, whatever, even if not in this life then in next birth.

Karmic account means a connection with any soul with whom we have had an earlier energy exchange. All our family and friends today are souls whom we have met in earlier lives. When we met before there was a relationship experience and an energy exchange. In the present life our relationship will be largely influenced by our past experiences.

There will be some souls who will do a lot for us and we do nothing much for them. There will be some for whom we do a lot and get nothing in return. There will be some who will create obstacles in our life. All their present experiences are a carry forward of the past energy exchanged with them.

Every human being loves children. We have to look into the reason of it. We normally feel that since we do not have conflict of interest with them we love. But as a matter of fact it is because children have only love for everybody. He is not finding any fault with anybody. He is not judgmental for anybody. He is constantly radiating love for everybody because his energy field is full of love only. For radiating love you can be natural if you keep yourself away from criticizing anybody or finding fault with anybody. It will remove your blockage of love and love will start flowing naturally for everybody. Children have full energy of love, they radiate love everywhere and bring others around also to their natural energy of love. Soul is so powerful; it comes out of all our layers. Children are fully charged with love so his vibrations charge everyone around with love. We have not to work for creating love we originally have love. The only thing we have to remove our blockages.

A baby does not see people through their labels of relationship, profession or status. A baby is not judgmental or critical about people. Hence a baby naturally radiates love since it has a soul to soul connection.

Love flows naturally through us if we remove the blocks created by ego labels, criticism, blame, control comparison and competition. We are shifting from ego consciousness to soul consciousness. Love radiating from us naturally emerges the original sanskar of love in every soul we interact with. We like going to places and meeting people who have pure vibrations because they emerge our own sanskar of purity. We are aware of the love, respect and care which we expect from others, we are aware of what we are getting and what we are not getting. Now we need to be aware of the love and care we are giving to others.

Sometimes, we part as partner in business or from any relationship. Before parting we may decide to part as friends. It is good but not enough. We have to erase bad thoughts for each other. We have to carry good thoughts; thoughts created for anybody reach to him. We should take responsibility of creating good thought for everybody, irrespective of other's creating howsoever negative thoughts for us. No doubt his negative thoughts will reach to us and naturally they will create negative thought in us, but we have to be aware and strong enough to take this responsibility of not creating negative thoughts for them.

When a group of people could be family and friends create similar thoughts for someone, then powerful collective vibrations get created and reach to the person. Positive vibrations can heal and negative vibrations can cause pain.

Since the creator and receiver are generally in a negative state of mind the effect of negative thoughts is faster. If we create pure thoughts for someone it will take sometimes for our positively to influence their mind.

Focus on seeing and retaining the good qualities in people. We see the weakness but take care not to churn it and consume negativity. Different souls have different Sanskars and so each soul's perspective and understanding of right and wrong will be different. What we find wrong in their behaviour may be right and justified by them.

Points to ponder:

- Shift the mind from self pity/self-criticism to self awareness and self evaluation when we criticize our self; we are reaffirming that we are weak and we are giving permission to our self to repeat the mistake.

- Never compare yourself with someone. You have to create beautiful relationship with yourself to have good relationship with others. Relationship with you should be good and powerful.

- Take responsibility for whatever thoughts you are creating. Don't just try to control your mind. When we try to control we blame others for creation of our thoughts. Create thought consciously and like to act on it finding it useful for you.

- Complaining depletes our energy because we are thinking about that which is not in our control. Complaining means focusing on the problem and concern is focusing on the solution.

- If we want to give light to others we have to glow ourselves. What we think we become. Altering of habits is a journey. We can change if we are aware, attentive and conscious of our behaviour inside the house, our own room, not only outside where we behave differently.

- We make certain image of ourselves and expect others to recognize it and respect that image. We are actually begging respect. Change to the mode of giving and give love and respect to others and strengthen your energy to get good results.

- We have to alter our programming what people will say. We always feel that we are good only if people appreciate us.

- Sometimes, unintentionally we compete even with our children, thinking nobody can do what I can do. We should be aware that we should feel good if others do better than us.

- Every human being loves a baby. It is because he does not put labels of relationship, profession or status. He is not judgmental or critical about people. He naturally radiates love having soul to soul connection.

- Whenever we part as partners in business or relationship, we should part as friends. But even it is not enough; we have to erase bad thoughts for each other and carry good thoughts.

MINDFUL PARENTING

Quote from Gary Smalley

"Affirming words from Moms and dads are like light switches, speak a word of affirmation at the right moment in a child's life and it is lighting up a whole roomful of possibilities".

Quote from Parikshit Jobanputra

"Parenting is a partnership with the God. You are working with the creator of the universe in shaping his creation (the child). So be graceful and careful".

Love of Parents towards children is natural. But parenting is an art. It has to be learnt. People learn it mostly from their own parents. We all want our children to be happy and successful. By success we mean material success. Parents have to make their children feel that they exist. Parents can only guide and not decide their destiny. Children only come through parents not from them. They are not parent's property or future investment. They have come in the form of life may be as your children. Parents try their best to make them dependent on them and do not want to liberate them. Parents want them to get attached to them. Before producing the children parents should be sure that they want to produce something better than them. For this parents have to be 100% straight.

Don't do parenting. Children need a friend and not a boss. The only qualification parents have is that they have come to this world a few years earlier than their children. Simply parents have to guide children before anybody on the street guides them. So the first thing children will have to be made free from any sort of fear so that they may come to parents for any advice. Parents are not the owner of children. Parents have simply provided children some substance of their genes. They have not provided them life. Parents have a privilege to make a better human being. So parents have to raise themselves before they raise their kids. Parents have to enjoy the privilege with responsibility. Don't expect children to become like you. Allow them to expand; don't restrict, make them responsible. It is better to let them experience in the protective boundaries rather than on the street.

The mother should not take any negative information through TV, news, violent or horror movies of loud music. The parents should meditate together to create healthy vibrations for the child. If parents create thoughts of anxiety about their capacity to bring up a child or about gender preference, they send vibrations of rejection to the child, and the child feels unwanted. A baby is old soul in a new body, which has been on a journey for many births. A baby's behaviour is because of the conditioning and experiences of the past birth. In a few years past memories will get deleted and present condition will take over. We need to take care of the present environment and vibrations. Parents need to give maximum affection to their children up to the age of 5. The first 5 years of child are the period of maturation of the brain and the body. If they are free from any pressures to achieve or compete at this time, then they experience a natural growth. If they are pulled into different directions then the brain is not able to grow naturally.

After the age of 5 parents have to teach their children values and discipline. While doing so they should be firm but should never beat their children. To make the children emotionally healthy and happy, the parents need to be emotionally strong. Emotional intelligence cannot be taught; parents have to have that to empower child. Having meals while, watching TV is not healthy for the mind and the body. We need to take care of - what we eat, when we eat and in what state of mind we eat, because you are what you eat. To heal the children if they are in pain, parents need to be stable, loving and powerful. If the parents come in pain, then they are only adding pain to the pain of the child. Children should play outdoor games with the objective of having fun, not to achieving something. If children are engaged in a lot of activities aiming for their future, it reflects sense of insecurity in the parents and sowing seeds of insecurity in the child.

Having our belief system that honesty does not work; we try to teach child to be honest. There is a conflict in our belief and words. So the message will reach to the child in a confused manner and it will have no impact. Actually the thought process is more powerful than words. This is the reason many a times parents feel, that they are teaching all sorts of good things to children but they don't understand or learn. We do differently and say different things to children. If we want to give good Sanskars to a child; we want him to be honest and should speak truth; we have to appreciate his honesty and truth speaking, if he tells honestly that he has not completed his homework or his duty to you, his honesty should not invoke you to speak against him. Parents need to check their belief systems, because children adopt the same belief systems and then it becomes their life and their destiny shapes accordingly. When we communicate we should say and do only what we firmly believe. If our belief system is different from our words, it sends a conflicting message to others, and then we complain that they do not understand us.

Our thoughts radiate continuously and words are used rarely. Thought energy travels faster than words. Therefore, thought communication is faster and more powerful than words and actions. Appreciate children for their values and let them grow up with the belief system that values work and are appreciated by the world, rather than focusing only on performance to get acceptance.

Many times children have to hide many things because of fear of their parents getting angry; if they tell them. The child is carrying the guilt and we are weakening him and are giving him a sanskar of hiding things. If the child gets success in hiding his wrong doings from his parents he develops a Sanskar and starts thinking him smart.

When we criticize or feel bad about our children; compare with other children and look down upon our children, we are depleting our children's energy and developing inferiority complex in him. When we always find fault with child and tell him he is wrong. Gradually he will start thinking that parents are wrong. Because whatever he is doing is according to his perspective right. When it happens, we say it is generation Gap. It is not generation Gap; both have to understand each other's perspective.

When we criticize our children, we are introducing him to him and he creates those impressions for himself and they carry with them and develop belief that they are like that. So, for whole life you are making him victim of it. So, we have not to criticize ourselves and our children but love and analyze to improve. What parents say about the child is an introduction that the child gets about himself. The child uses the opinion of the parents to create an image about him.

Comparison - Out of our love for children we develop comparison in him for his improvement. Comparison is as bad as criticism. There may be quiet children having fear and quiet as his nature. We have to accept him as a soul with past Sanskars. They have not to be ridiculed or criticized. We come across with lots of children with completely different nature as compared to their families. It is all the reason of past Sanskars. Every child's relationship with parents is also affected by their old Sanskars.

In each birth the Soul has had different parents, environment and situations and so different Sanskars. The soul carrying Sanskars of so many births comes as a child and we expect the child to be like the parents. Sanskars of the family do influence the child, but most of the Sanskars will be what they have carried from previous lives.

Comparison between siblings causes the child to feel that the parents love his sibling more than him. This causes low self esteem and sibling rivalry. When we want someone to change their sanskars, we need to empower them. Empowerment comes from appreciating and highlighting their beautiful Sanskars

When a child performs or shows his achievements everyone appreciates him and calls him a good child. At that age we develop the belief that when we perform and people appreciate then we are good person. When a child made a mistake everyone criticized the doer and not the deed. Our self esteem became dependent on public opinion i.e., if people appreciate us then we are a good person if people criticize us we are a bad person.

When people have the faith that we will not react but will respond with understanding, they are ready to tell us truth. Dishonesty is used because of fear of anger. Punishment, anger and reactive behaviour dis-empower a child, because we are radiating negative energy. Discipline means empowerment and transformation, so that they do not make the mistake again, this requires the energy of love and understanding.

Two souls born in the same family carry different Sanskars of the past births, and so they are two different personalities. Comparing them and asking one to be like the other, lowers the self esteem of the child. Comparison and criticism dis-empower people.

Every statement we are making for a child whether in thoughts or in words, he is using that to create his self image, and this will be the basis of his self esteem. We need to use only positive and powerful thoughts and words when we communicate with our children.

Parents should not thrust their decision on children but try to convince them to make their own decisions. If we thrust he will never take responsibility of that decision and the consequences of that decision will remain on the mind of child for ever as he will always think that it was not his decision. Parents should make it sure that child acts on his own decisions. Parents may counsel but ultimately it has to be the decision of the child. Whatever the child does at that time they are right from their perspective. The parents may not agree with the child but need to accept that the child has a reason for what he is doing. This gives the child acceptance and respect.

If the parents always feel that the child is wrong, then that sends a feeling of rejection. At the same time there are friends who will accept and the child will drift towards peer pressure. Feeling of rejection created in a child becomes the sanskar of his soul. Then even in other relationships whether at home, work or friends, the individual tends to feel unwanted. Our Sanskars influence our thinking patterns. Every time we respond in the same manner, we are deepening the Sanskar. Then the slightest stimulus creates the same response.

The child then forces himself to do even that what he does not want to do, so that he does not lose the acceptance of friends. Your self esteem has become dependent on people's acceptance, and hence we are always concerned about what do people think about us. While taking decisions it is important to only remember what is good for you and your family and what is in our capacity, rather than pleasing people to feel happy.

Parents normally tell children that they are in pain because of some of their actions and think this will change the children. It gives children pain and guilt. He is pained as he has given pain to the parents and thinking himself guilty of it. It depletes child's strength and gives him a feeling of guilt. It will in no way help him to gather strength. In such cases if parents change themselves and don't create pain and try to bring the change with love, it will heal the parents and release the pressure of child. We should not think and want children to be as we want them to become. We may be right as per our perception and not as per their perception.

Supposing your child does not get good marks and you feel sorry and upset. We should be aware that if we are sorry or upset the child will also be upset. My responsibility is to give positive mind to child and to raise status of his mind. My prime responsibility is to take measures to see that in future child gets good marks. By getting upset we are depleting our energy, his energy and giving child a feeling that we are unhappy because of you. We are not proud of you. Children commit suicide not because they have failed in their exams but because they are unable to face their parents. They feel that they have not made their parents happy and proud. It is our responsibility to see that we are not creating constant stress and competitiveness. Criticism depletes children's physical, intellectual, emotional and spiritual health. They should be equally balanced.

We should make him not only physically or intellectually strong, but we should also make him emotionally and spiritually strong. (IQ, EQ and SQ - Intelligent, emotional and spiritual). We have to make our child very good human being, emotionally and spiritually strong along with intellectually and physically. Most of the times, we don't realize that our responsibility is to make our children emotionally and spiritually strong. It's time to do now and think on those lines.

Parents should be careful that they have to increase the strength of child. If the child takes some decision and goes with it the parents should support and send positive feelings wishing him all good for his decision. The parents should not wait to see that the child's decision may go wrong and then they can prove their point that their decision was wrong and whatever they were saying was correct and they are facing the consequence of their doing. Children should also see the love behind any advice of the parents. Main thing is love, acceptance and respect between the relationships.

When the child seeks support he prefers to go to friends, friend's parents or professional counselor. It is because when the child approaches to others, he expects acceptance and love. He will go only where he can get love, acceptance and compassion. When a person is in pain, may be your own child, needs love, acceptance and support not anger or non acceptance and searching for reason. First thing required is to give him strength to bear that pain not as guilt but as a mistake. Then we can counsel him. So first we will have to prepare him to accept our counseling.

When someone shares their problem or mistake with a counselor, the counselor is detached and stable. Being stable means the mind is not critical or judgmental. Family and friends on hearing the mistake get critical, angry, hurt or even feel let down. With all these emotions the energy of love and care gets blocked.

Sometimes parents find some gap between relationship with their children when they become grown up and mature. The parents should first understand that it may be because of past Janam Karmas and should start having positive feelings for the children. Forgetting all past they should remove the blockages and start having positive feelings for them. Children always have the belief that parents never intended to do anything bad to them. But because of many reasons they develop a feeling that they are not accepted by their parents as they are and this creates gap in the relationship. Both have to forget the past taking as past karmik and now start accepting each other and send positive thoughts to each other. This should be unconditional with the feeling that we are doing for ourselves and not for others.

Even if we have been critical or rejecting our child earlier, it is time to now change the energy we sent them and start healing them. Their Sanskars of hurt and rejection are deep but when we change the quality, the process of change begins.

Children always need to remember their parents were never wrong. They may have made mistakes, but their intention was always pure and the best for the child.

Siblings should not compare the relationships the parents have with them. Each One's relationship and therefore the energy exchange is a carry forward of a past karmic account and is largely influenced by the quality of exchange earlier.

This is a matter of concern that formerly women use to cook like their mothers and now they drink like their fathers. Addiction for anything weakens the will power. It brings change in one's behaviour and thinking. So the parents out of their love feel pained when they see the behaviour of their children changing. This may develop in anger and then hatred. We have to change our thinking and instead of being angry see the reasons for this change.

When the children feel neglected or rejected they develop addiction just to draw the attention of their parents and sometimes even for punishing the parents. When someone gets addicted to a substance their will power starts reducing because of the dependency and this lowers the self esteem of the individual, and creates pain, anger and frustration in them. This brings about a personality change. Children can take to substance abuse to get attention from their parents. It can also be a subtle way of causing pain to their parents. The child holds them responsible for the pain he went through because of criticism, neglect or rejection.

A person who is addicted has a negative self image. Family's negative image about them reaffirms their self image and depletes the strength needed to overcome the addiction. The negative vibrations received lower the self esteem and therefore are an obstacle in letting the person overcome the addiction not behaviour. It does not mean we encourage them to consume it but it only means we do not create any thoughts of anger, pain or hurt.

It is general belief system that relations between the girl and in laws will have some or other glitches. This belief system creates negative feelings from the beginning. We have to develop a thinking that some soul is coming to our family. So we have to change the label from relationship to the truth.

Whenever we create a relationship let the consciousness be, it is a connection between two souls. If we are in the consciousness of the labels like mother in law, daughter in law then we are not creating good energy because of the beliefs attached with the labels.

Generally after the marriage of children parents feel that children are more involved with their new partner or relationship and are not spending time with them. So parents feel emotionally difference in the behaviour. It is because of our attachment and expectations. If we create negative thoughts about the child they will be more painful. If we think they have just entered in new relationship and may not be able to give the required love to their new relationship. So instead of expecting from them we should think of giving to them more.

When there is attachment we fear that the other person is moving away and getting attached to someone else. We feel our happiness is moving away. When there is love there is no fear. When there is a change outside we need to accept and adopt by bringing about a change inside, if we do not change inside then we are resisting the outer change, and sending vibrations of resistance and rejection. When we send energy of resistance people move away. The same people whom we want should be close to us be with us move away from us because of the energy of pain they are getting from us.

Children today are going through their own stresses of managing their work and family. Parents have always given them love, support and power. Parents can continue giving them the same instead of expecting emotional support from them. When parents start feeling neglected they create pain and add to the pain of the child. If the parents can take care of their state of being and continue giving love and support they will empower their children.

In case of daughter getting married we are worried about her life. We feel attached emotionally and give all sorts of negative thoughts. We give thought to the daughter that her parents are always right and she has to meet now parent in laws to whom she does not know. This is very damaging and creates lots of problems. She explains her problems to her parents and goes back to in laws home with that feeling. Parents have to be stable. They can't be either strong or weak. They have to be stable and get unattached. No bias should be formed. If parents have slightest bias they will always think that their daughter is right.

I will like to share with you my personal experience of a real incident.

"One of my friend's daughter got married to a boy of her choice. Parents of daughter somehow were not in favor of that marriage. But because of pressure from the daughter the marriage was performed. Later on, after about three years of marriage differences between girl and boy and both the families reached to a point where divorce happened. The girl had a baby girl of one year and she had come along with the baby to her parent's home. After a few days because of social pressure and may be from her parents also the guilt feeling was created in the girl's mind. As a consequence the girl committed suicide. The matter took very ugly shape and both families suffered for many years, remained in pain and all sorts of mental agony. Ultimately spirituality healed them and they could accept the situation and came out of their pain".

In such circumstances we have to take a detached view. Detachment means that I am separate from the body, role and responsibility. If the connection is label to label then it is attachment. When we are detached we are stable in our interactions. When there is attachment we get emotionally disturbed in response to other's pain. We are not able to see the things in the right perspective and take accurate decision.

We should not worry if people are not listening to us but we should worry that they are watching us. Children will develop the same attitude, what we have towards them. They don't learn what you tell them but they learn from what you are. What you are doing, how you are behaving. If you say something and do something else, the energy field is created in children is what you are doing. People teach children to respect people working for them but they themselves don't respect the people working for them; children will never learn to respect others. We teach to children not to fear from certain thing of which we fear. We believe that our saying will have more effect than our behaviour because they do not understand what we are doing; they understand what we say to them. We will have to change this belief system. Whatever, we want to teach children or others first we have to practice that in our life.

Children are always influenced by our attitude. Our attitude created by our belief systems and thought process create our energy field and vibrations. Our vibrations become a part of our child's vibrations and their vibrations develop their attitude.

Points to ponder

- When the child is in womb the mother should not take any negative information through TV, news, violent or horror movies and loud music. To make the child emotionally healthy and happy the parents need to be emotionally strong.

- There should be no conflict in parent's belief and words. Actually the thought process is stronger than words. Parents need to check their belief systems because whatever we say children adopt that as their belief system.

- Always appreciate children for their values and let them grow up with the belief system that values are appreciated by the world rather than focusing only on performance to get acceptance.

- Never criticize your children. When we are criticizing our children we are making them victim in their eyes for their entire life. We should analyze their deficiencies with love to improve.

- We should not inculcate the habit of comparison and competition in the child. We should make them free from any pressures to achieve or compete to enable his brain to grow naturally. Comparison is as bad as criticism.

- Punishment, anger and reactive behavior dis-empower a child because we are radiating the negative energy. Discipline means empowerment and transformation so that they do not make the mistake again.

- Parents should not thrust their decision on children but try to convince them to make their own decision. Let parents empower children to walk the path and strengthen them to cross any obstacle that comes on the way.

- Don't make child feel guilty that parents are upset or in pain because of some of his acts. They have the responsibility to give positive mind to the child and to raise status of his mind.

- Parents have to make their children good human being, emotionally and spiritually strong along with intellectually and physically.

- Sometimes parents don't approve and accept their children's views and force them to accept what they feel right as per their perspective. They are actually reducing the strength of their children.

- In case of daughter getting married parents are normally worried of her life. We have general belief system that girl is going to a new house. We feel attached emotionally. Parents of daughter have to be stable. They have to get unattached. No bias should be formed.

MIND YOUR OWN BUSINESS

In every situation instead of checking what is right for the situation or the other person first take care of what is the right way for you to be in the situation. To take controls of the situation first take control of you. Going out of control, means disconnected from your natural self of purity, peace, love and happiness. One wrong has no right to correct another wrong and has no power to change them. We have to be in the right before inspiring others to change.

There was once a pair of acrobats. The teacher was a poor widower and the student was a young girl by the name of Meda. These acrobats performed each day on the streets in order to earn enough to eat.

Their act consisted of the teacher balancing a tall bamboo pole on his head while the little girl climbed slowly to the top. Once to the top, she remained there while the teacher walked along the ground.

Both performers had to maintain complete focus and balance in order to prevent any injury from occurring and to complete the performance. One day, the teacher said to the pupil:

'Listen Meda, I will watch you and you watch me, so that we can help each other maintain concentration and balance and prevent an accident. Then we'll surely earn enough to eat.'

But the little girl was wise, she answered, 'Dear master, I think it would be better for each of us to watch our self. To look after one self means to look after both of us. That way I am sure we will avoid any accidents and earn enough to eat.'

We have a basic instinct of observation. Just immediately, the child is Born, he/she starts observing his mother and then others. Since, childhood, we make it our SANSKAR to observe our mother, father and others. Since, at that time child does not have thinking power, it becomes his SANSKAR. This process continues till he/she acquires thinking power.

Once the child starts thinking his observations become subjective. Child starts applying his mind and starts discriminating what is right and what is wrong according to his/her thinking. Later, child develops his own experiences, thinking and so forms habits justifying his acts based on his experiences and thinking. So, he starts becoming critical and starts analyzing what others are doing, what according to him is good to emulate or what is wrong others are doing. Then based on thinking which is made out of his experiences and observations he starts thinking what is right and what is wrong. So he starts becoming judgmental.

In this whole process, he forgets, when he has become so critical that all the time he is noticing others, what they are doing, what they are wearing, what they are eating and what they are saying, how they are behaving etc. On the top of this he also starts guessing as to what they are thinking about me and my behaviour.

So instead of focusing on our self we start spending our energy on others. We stop thinking, what we want, what we are doing or what we should do. We become stagnant and start depleting gradually.

We gradually, develop believing that what we are doing is right and with all good intentions start thinking that others should also behave in the same manner. We honestly start feeling that it is our duty to correct everything around us to make a better society.

In the process, we become so intent that we feel why others are not behaving as they should behave. We start feeling that we control the whole world and they all should behave and act as I think better and we start believing that it is only good for them. We want others to be perfect finished product as per our perception, whereas, we think for ourselves as human being not expected to be perfect. To err is human. We have image of perfection which we colour with our colour. We can't see other's sincerity if we have a habit of doubt. We will think he must be doing it for some of his benefit.

We have to develop Sanskar of seeing everybody as they are and love them as they are. We normally carry a preconceived image of how we want particular person or a particular relationship to be. We then keep comparing the person to the image in our mind and try to make them like the image we created.

Quote from J Krishnmurty

"In oneself lies the whole world and if you know how to look and learn, the door is there and the key is in your hand. Nobody on earth can give you either the key or the door to open, except yourself".

What a myth. We completely forget that we have no control on others. They will behave and act as they feel correct for them. We unknowingly start writing script of others. When we realize, we can't change them as per our wish, we increase our pain and start thinking negative of them. They have no brains. They don't know how to behave. They are not fit to live in a civilized community. All sorts of negative thoughts start coming in our mind. It all is reflected on our face and behaviour. So, we create the whole atmosphere of negativity. We completely forget our goal of life. We lose focus on our doings. We forget what we want to achieve and end up just teaching others, on whom we have no control. They are least bothered about what we are telling them and have no respect for us and our saying. Ultimately, we don't affect other's behaviour and lose our energy on other's on whom we have no control.

For us to grow in spirit, it is we who must change and not the people, places or things around us. The only given we have in our lives is OURSELVES and that is the only factor we have control over. When we change who and what we are within our heart our life follows suit and changes too.

We should be aware and keep on reminding us that people and situations will not move or act as per our thinking of right or wrong. So instead, of finding fault in others we should seize it as an opportunity to increase our tolerance. We should make ourselves so strong and powerful that actions of others or situation will not affect or hurt us. On every step we should be aware that instead of following others we should search for our happiness. We know for sure, that we can't change others but we can always control our mind, of which, we are the sole owners.

I have to narrate a personal story to you:-

"My spiritual Guru Sadhguru Sri Rameshji always says, whatever Gyan your are getting here in Satsang don't just go and start preaching others. Once in his spiritual

retreat in Himalayas one lady was criticizing her husband vehemently and was asking how to correct her husband. Guruji gave her first advise don't tell your husband about any Gyan which you have got here. Actually, we have to practice this Gyan and show others the changes we have made in ourselves. Our Gyan will not change others unless they want to change. We have to change and set example".

When we observe a weakness or a wrong act of another person we start churning on it. It stays on our mind for a long time and soon becomes a part of our memory so other's negativity becomes a part of our mind and intent. When we keep other's negativity on our mind, then we can never become perfect and cannot be happy. So, we should be aware and practice, all the time that even while witnessing negative SANSKAR or a wrong KARMA of others, we should not absorb it on our mind. When, we absorb someone's weakness in thoughts, it will definitely come into our words someday somewhere. It is bound to come. Our mind is trained to come out somewhere, whatever it has absorbed of someone. Speaking ill about someone will return like an Echo, louder and more in magnitude. They will criticize and speak ill about us more than we did about them. Later on, we will realize but damage is done. That is a vicious circle. Your this habit may create lots of enemies in the society, contrary to this if you appreciate others it will create more and more friends for you. Everybody has some or the other good quality, observe that and absorb that in your mind and then let appreciation come out of your mind genuinely and then see its effect. You will always be surrounded by nice genuine persons in a most positive and peaceful atmosphere.

Going a step forward if someone is speaking ill about some other person, even slight supporting them, endorsing what they are saying, we become a part of their KARMIC pattern. So, we need to take care that we don't support another's negative KARMA because the moment we support that KARMA, we become a part of that and it becomes our KARMA.

Spiritually speaking- People cannot be the way we wanted them to be. First we should ask ourselves, are we ready to be as people want us to be. Everyone will be the way he wants to be. It is universal truth everyone will be as per their SANSKARS with which they have come and have been brought up. Once we accept it we can end our irritation. When we accept it we can be courteous to ourselves by not creating negative thoughts for those who are not behaving as we would like them to behave. If anybody in your opinion, not behaving or saying as you think proper, don't give him negative thoughts, but relax him, empower him, laugh it out and say ok. Your positive thoughts for him in this process will reach to him. We will be first cool and then cool him also.

We sometimes feel that we can change the habits of people. So when we find any people's habit as per our perspective wrong we wish to change it for his good. In Spite of our best efforts, people may not agree for change because they are comfortable with their habits and find nothing wrong into it. It happens because our and their perspective of right or wrong can be different. So we have to understand their perspective also before advising. We have not to take a judgmental view and be critical about people even in our thoughts and start criticizing others. Criticism of others will deplete our power and will create negativity in our thoughts which will reach to others and they will start thinking negative about us, which will further deplete our power. So instead of our advice having any effect on them a vicious circle of negative conversation between the two minds will start and will harm both as well as the society at large, instead of doing any good to either.

While listening sometimes we develop the habit of focusing on the purpose of the person speaking and do not listen what he is saying. We may actually be listening but we do not get the substance of the message which the speaker is trying to convey but we waste our time in just focusing on the object or the purpose of the speaker, which ultimately is of no use to us. So in fact we are concentrating on the messenger rather than the message.

Some people develop habit of preparing themselves for the answer to the thing which they are listening. In that process they actually do not listen what the speaker is speaking but he is just concentrating on what he has to say after the speaker finishes his talk. So he is actually listening but does not get anything in the listening. A good listener is not one who simply listens and does not speak in between, but a good listener is one who is focusing, while listening, on the matter and substance which the speaker is trying to convey.

There is a teacher sitting inside us, but we are unable to listen to him, because we have created much noise in our minds. We have to observe silence, everyday, for some moments, to listen the command of our teacher sitting inside i.e., intuition or conscience what is right for me is within me and more we listen to our inner teacher, we would be better off.

Professional supervision of people's working for us is different than to observe others for finding fault with them. We have to accept and respect the people working along with us and then we should observe them professionally and advice them. The other persons then will respect us and try to accept our advice. So if we want our advice to be respected we will have to respect other people, have to accept everybody and give them the confidence that whatever, you are saying is out of love and respect. It will not create any negativity and will not give you pain. It will not deplete your power of soul but contrary to that you will derive happiness by his accepting your advice and he is being benefitted by that will increase your power of the soul.

Points to ponder

- We should be aware whether we are becoming so critical that all the time we are noticing others. We are caring for other's opinion about our behaviour.

- We want others to be perfect finished product as per our perception. We start believing that whatever we are doing is correct and others should behave in the same manner.

- We should be always aware that people and situations will not move or act as per our thinking of right or wrong. Always remember that by trying to change others we are increasing our pain, reducing our strength and unnecessarily getting disturbed and hurt.

- If anybody in our opinion not behaving or speaking as per our thinking proper, we should not give negative thoughts to him but should relax him, empower him, laugh it away positively and say OK.

- Sometimes, with all good intentions we start taking it as our duty to correct everything around us to make a better society. But we forget that this thought is coming out of feeling of authority, whereas, we have no control on others.

- We unknowingly start writing of script of others on whom we have no control. We increase our pain, loose focus on our doings, deplete our energy and create the atmosphere of negativity all around.

IMPORTANCE OF GURU

Quote from Sri Sri Ravi Sankar

"A Guru is there to show you what you are. You are not different from me. Whatever I am, that is what you are. This is your highest possibility."

Guru Govind Dono Khade, Kake lagu pai
Balihari guru aapki, govind diyo bataye

In modern society many people believe that they do not need a Guru to become enlightened. We have to be realistic and think; can we achieve enlightenment without a Guru. If we have to learn anything, even alphabets, just think, could you learn these alphabets without the help of a Guru? One may be having all the parts of a machine but without the necessary skill he cannot fix the machine with those all parts.

Guru plays a vital role in our life. Guru is one who guides us from darkness to light. There are two worlds; one we can see and one which is not visible. It is Guru only who can show us what is not visible. Guru is sitting inside of everyone. But because of the worldly dust on our soul and eyes we do not listen to guru sitting inside us. Thus, an external Guru is required to make us listen to our Guru sitting inside.

The Bhagavad Gita is a dialogue where Krishna speaks to Arjuna of the role of a guru, and similarly emphasizes in verse 4.34 that those who know their subject well are eager for good students, and the student can learn from such a guru through reverence, service, effort and the process of inquiry.

A big conflict is always going on between mind and our consciousness. There is always a discussion and many a times we listen to our mind and disagree with our consciousness. Our consciousness is overpowered by our mind and we do think against our consciousness. Slowly, we reach to a point that our consciousness stops telling us and we become completely slave of our mind. Mind suggests the outwardly things which look very attractive and we get trapped. This is **'MAYA'** *(Illusion)*.To come out of this illusion, we need somebody to put brakes to it and bring us out of this darkness. This Sanskar becomes so strong that we stop listening not only to our consciousness but to people around us also; whosoever says anything against this. So, we are all the time surrounded by the people who say 'yes' to our mind and we get entangled more and more. We close all the doors from where we can get light and we start enjoying the darkness around us. We start thinking it light and our belief system becomes that anybody who is saying it dark is actually either don't understand it or saying out of his jealous that he could not get it. Thus, a living Guru is very important in our life.

This world is just a pilgrimage — of great significance, but not a place to belong to, not a place to become part of Remain a lotus leaf, as Kabir says.

When you are in full control of your mind, you feel and accept anything what is happening around you and you feel unaffected in a mindless state. In that state even a non-existent can become your Guru. But when you are full of mind you need another mind to fix you. You need another mind cleverer than you and unbiased to fix your mind. If you want to learn anything singing or sports you need a coach or Guru. So, if you want to know anything about spirituality, good or bad, you need a spiritual Guru. We need Guru at every stage of life. We may be very successful in our business or profession. We still hire advisor or consultant to improve our endeavor. We may have attained name and fame. We may always be receiving lots of appreciation from the people around us. There is a big challenge, when you are successful in life, because nothing succeeds like success. Everybody whosoever will be coming in contact with you will be speaking as per your mind. This will develop a feeling that whatever I think or do is correct. We will stop listening to others. We will not get the other's views and we will become stagnant. This is a state of mind when we require a Guru, who can always tell us our shortcomings and different points of views also. On the contrary, when you are facing difficulties and failure, you get dejected. At that stage, everybody around you starts criticizing and blaming your decisions and actions. You start believing in those criticisms and develop a feeling of guilt; start holding yourself responsible for everything happening around you not going in your favour. This state of mind leads you to depression. In this stage, it is only Guru, who can bring you out of depression with his karuna (Compassion) and blessings.

The word Guru is a very sacred word. But we find it very difficult to get a Guru. A Guru has to be such who has attraction of soul. Our soul should get attracted by someone to be our Guru. Our Guru should be accomplished individual in the field of spirituality to guide us to right path. We should have confidence in him that whatever he says is just out of love and selflessness. We should be able to develop unquestionable faith in him. We should be able to surrender completely to him and his word should be last word for us. We can be benefitted by Guru only if we have full faith and we have a feeling of complete surrender towards him.

The simple question arises in mind why we need Guru. When you are on an unknown journey you don't know so you need an instructor. When you are driving on an unknown path, you take the help of G.P.S, which can guide you. You believe G.P.S because you trust it. You have confidence in it. G.P.S is also Guru Processing system. Actually, what we do not know, Guru processes it for us and then guides us. Nowadays we have social media where we can listen to various Sadhgurus and can be benefitted. We require having living Guru who can reply and solve all our problems and doubts. He will bring us out from darkness to light.

Awareness is a process of being more and more awake.

What relationship we should have with Guru. A friend, parent or loved one.

A friend - We should feel about Guru as one in whom we can confide and put our complete trust. If Guru is friend, he is supposed to support you in your limitations and somebody who makes you comfortable. Somebody who attacks your ego you will never like him as friend. So Guru can't be a friend.

A parent - Our parents are not our choice. We cannot opt for our natural parents. Natural parents normally wish to experience everything in their children's life which they could not achieve in their life. So we can't take our natural parents as Guru who can be authoritarian. We cannot control people so we can't be authoritarian. Parents normally compare and create competition in children for their good. Guru does not want to compare between their disciples and Guru also does not teach their disciples to compete with anybody. Guru teaches disciple to compete with themselves only.

A loved one – We should make a GURU to whom we love, respect and trust. We can surrender to him completely.

What can we do for our Guru- Best thing we can do for our Guru what a garden can do for the gardener. The best thing you can do for anybody is to be as they want you to be. Best thing one can do for Guru; one has to be peaceful, prosperous and move ahead towards the path of spiritualism. Guru gives same thing to everybody but some receive it properly and some not. Guru does not want to settle for less or more but he wants to settle for the whole.

Even the most intimate and beautiful relationships with friends or parents will not get us to the ultimate goal of life which is salvation. Only a Guru can whose main job is to liberate his disciples.

We all suffer from mainly two types of diseases - one infectious and other internal. The infectious diseases are caused by the external factors and so they can be cured by external help i.e. doctors and medical science. The internal diseases are the diseases caused by ourselves. They may be genetic or the result of our life style or misuse of body and our strength. The internal diseases can be cured by internal doctor only. External doctors or medical science can only provide us help to tolerate that. The internal doctor is only one sitting inside us i.e. consciousness. Actually our consciousness is our Guru. But the worldly circumstances and situations have depleted our strength to adhere to our consciousness. Here there is a need of somebody who can strengthen us to adhere to our consciousness. Guru is the

God sent doctor to make ourselves aware of our consciousness and remove our internal diseases.

As a matter of fact nobody can explain the importance of Guru fully. Can we in any way gauze the importance of some power somewhere creating, managing and destroying the whole universe? There is some power which is balancing the whole universe. How and why we have come in this universe, we don't know. We need somebody who can explain this to us. It is Guru only, because he has experienced it through his **SADHNA** and **TAPASYA.**

Points to ponder

- Guru guides us from darkness to light. Guru shows us what is not visible to us.
- We are under illusion of the worldly attractions. Guru puts brakes to it and brings us out of this illusion (darkness).
- We can be benefitted by Guru only if we have full faith and a feeling of complete surrender towards him.
- Guru is GPS (Guru Processing System); what we do not know Guru processes it for us and then guides us.
- Guru is a God sent doctor to make ourselves aware of our consciousness and remove our internal diseases.

RELATIONSHIP

Quote from SadhGuruRameshJI

" One single thread doesn't has enough strength but when some threads are twisted together and made into a rope, the combined strength increases thousand times more than the total strength of all the threads"

Quote by Zen Meditation Practitioner
Aditya Ajmera Ji

"Everything in the universe exists in relationship to something. Nothing exists in isolation. We live in a wonderful world that is full of cosmic connectivity and synchronicity. Journey of life is best measured in LIVING NOW, SEEING NOW, KNOWING NOW, ACCEPTING NOW, BEING NOW & DIEING NOW."

Relationships are never absolute they are variable in nature. The absolute relationship can only be with the dead or nonexistent i.e., GOD. People do what they want to do; they don't do what you want them to do. Relationships have to be conducted right all the time. The moment they are not conducted properly they can always go haywire. Relationship has to be coming together and sharing not extracting. We feel cheated when we are denied of something for which we had the illusion. If illusion is broken; think it is bringing you near to the reality.

Love is homely and ordinary, expressed not in grand proclamations but in our everyday activities. It's how we hold one another just so, in full awareness there's nothing to hold on to. Love is unstoppable because it is ungraspable:

> *When looked at, nothing to see.*
> *When listened to, nothing to hear.*
> *When used, nothing to use up.*
> *Hence, inexhaustible.*
> *(Tao Te Ching, verse 35)*

Love is an art just as living is an art. If we want to learn how to love we must proceed in the same way like we want to learn any other art say music or painting. But most of us see love as an acquisition rather than art; like a new phone which we gaze at reverently as we take it out from the box and gently cradle in our hands. The first time it falls there is an anguished gasp. We snatch it from the ground, meticulously examine it for small scuffs and carefully put it back in our pockets. Soon we begin tossing it around unperturbed by the falls and tumbles. One fine day we look at the scratches and dents, and murmur to ourselves, perhaps it's time to get a new one again.

Humans are called social animals. We as human being believe in relationships. Our very birth is the outcome of a relationship. We get relationships in place right from our birth. Certain relationships we have through birth and then we develop further relationships with the people we come across during our life. Everybody understands the value of relationships. It is the biggest treasure of ours. We have to maintain it. It cannot be earned easily. We have to be very vigilant and conscious in maintaining these relationships.

Relationships are of various types some are blood relationships some are offshoots of the family and some are formed during the course of journey of our life when we come in touch with various people in various fields. All relationships are precious. We, for our happiness, take care to maintain our relationships. We should not be guided by the short term benefits through relationships. We should always be prepared to do the required sacrifice, to the extent we can afford for maintaining the relationship. We should always be aware to address if anything is coming in between the relationship.

Best relationship is not the one which brings together the perfect people. But relationship requires each individual to learn to live with imperfection of others. One should learn to admire other person's values and qualities. Relationship is not between two concrete blocks which will break just by small friction. Relationship and love can be there when you fall in it. Meaning thereby you will have to drop something for keeping your relationship. Relationship requires adjustment.

In relationship, one should always be conscious to do what he wants from others to do and give. But don't expect from others what you do for them. Relationship should be based on intentions and not words. It should be based on feelings and vibrations. Relationships are based on strong ties, but are very tender in nature. Relationships take it for granted that we respect each other and love each other. There cannot be any relationship where both don't have respect and love for each other. Since, mutual respect and love are the basis of relationship, we have to be careful and aware all the time that we don't do or say any such thing which may hurt the other person. But in relationship, many a times it may so happen that the other person feels hurt by your behaviour and you may feel that you have not done anything wrong which may hurt him. In such cases, if intentions are right, then each one of you can get over this hurt.

But these are tender moments and we have to take care that these small hurts may not lead to moving away from the relationships. We should always make our utmost efforts to get over from the hurt, because even if we move away from the relationship we would be carrying the hurt which will constantly cause damage to our happiness.

Some people have SANSKARS to speak to others in such a way which they never want others to talk to them or speak to them. Some have SANSKARS of getting a feeling of being insulted very quickly and they create hurt in themselves because of that. We may be having either or both SANSKARS and a SANSKAR of seeing both from the same lens. We have to think and accept that this is my SANSKAR and I have to change it. It is ultimately, because we are so attached to certain things or way that we always want them to happen as we wish. We are normally attached to certain image that how people should think. Actually, these images are not real. We have created these images and they are main reason of our hurt. We should be aware that others may be having other image and they are acting according to that image.

Relationship is not a give and take as it pleases you. While, we are consciously acting or talking to a person beyond our reach even in anger, we don't utter bad words, because we are consciously not permitting our mind to use any foul language, but when we have no fear of the other person or we consciously permit our mind to use foul language, we utter bad words and then we forgive us that it happened in heat of moment. We have to be aware of it all the time in our relationships.

Relationship based on love and respect has a spark which can never be extinguished. We may feel strain or dint in the relationship because of any circumstance or situation. We may have developed that strain to the extent of utmost hatred and not seeing face to face. But very small gesture or initiation from any one of them may ignite that love again and bring back even more love. Always keep in mind that at the time when you are having strained relation with a person, whom you have loved, you don't say or do any such thing which may kill that spark, which may bounce back at any time of need in life. Always be first to take first step of that gesture or initiative which may ignite that spark of love in the relationship. Don't wait for other to take that step. Your first step will give you immense happiness and even if relationship is not restored, you will have the happiness of at least trying from your side. Don't lose faith in your honest intention.

Respect is:

- *Love without attachment, Acceptance without judgment.*
- *Surrender without giving up, Admiration without hype.*
- *Appreciation without expectations,*
- *And all respect starts with: Self-respect*

I will like to share with you my personal experience of a real incident.

"There were two real brothers, who because of some circumstances had become daggers drawn with each other. Once it so happened that both of them went to attend a funeral on the bank of Ganges in North India in the month of January. The cold breeze was blowing. One elder brother was having a woolen shawl and the other brother was just wearing a pullover and was feeling intense cold. The elder brother having a woolen shawl could not see his brother shivering and shouted at younger brother that he is shivering but could not come to me and sit in the shawl. He took him

in the shawl and embraced. They forgot everything and again became same brothers with full of love and respect for each other".

Trust is the greatest binding force in the relationship. It should be first thing in the relationship and be conscious all the time that it should be the last thing to go in a relationship. As a matter of fact trust should never ever finish. Normally trust comes very late and it is the first thing to go. Whenever, we develop a feeling in a relationship that we cannot trust him again, we actually fear the hurt, which we can create out of our thinking that the other person can do the same thing again, which we don't expect. We don't fear trusting them but we fear our getting hurt by them. If we think that they cannot hurt; if I don't create hurt then we can give others more chance and believe in most of the cases. We will find that we will not be disappointed.

When we doubt people around us and in society or at the workplace then doubting becomes our SANSKAR and then it becomes difficult to trust even family friends and other relations. We should not stop trusting people because of fear of getting hurt. The best way is to communicate with them rather than stop talking. I feel differently and I wish you could have behaved differently forget and forgive. Either, he will change or you will start thinking differently so that you don't feel hurt. Once you accept that he wants to act differently and then you will be able to deal him accordingly and not get hurt.

We should always be aware that it is not difficult to maintain relationships. Only thing required is love and trust. We should deal with love and trust. Be always ready to forget and forgive. People develop a nature where they don't love anybody. It may be the outcome of their experience where the response to their love might have hurt them. They have to think that their response didn't hurt they hurt themselves. So they can remove the fear of getting hurt again and love will start flowing. One has to prepare himself that other's response will not hurt him. Relationship is necessary because unless we have somebody to whom we can give love we can't get love, neither from him nor from inside.

Keeping doubt is depleting the energy and base of relationship on fragile ground. Trust is the original Sanskar, shall create love and shall remain connected. One, who does not believe, has labeled the other person.

When Computer is hung, CTRL+ALT+DEL, similarly when life is hung, when your close relationship is strained; control, alter and delete your negativity. Create positive thoughts for each other; believe me your life and relationship will again start flowing with love and happiness.

Sometimes we feel that the daily routine and same process is very boring and painful. We cannot change the process but we can change our awareness. The process is not painful but we create pain. We have not to stop the storm but we have to save ourselves from that storm. In relationship if the other is wrong we collide and try to correct him rather than taking care of ourselves and gently influence the other by our thinking. Taking care of ourselves is spirituality.

Sometimes our relations get strained as we are still remembering past. We are becoming judgmental and we are scared of future threats. We don't forget and forgive the past incidents and create barriers. We are not able to let it go. We can do it by just simply thinking that pain was created by me. We create our expectations we decide they are not met and then we create pain that the other person is not meeting my expectations. In fact we find people very judgmental.

We also become judgmental and start liking and disliking other's actions. We have to be aware that each one has his own way and we should not put labels and be judgmental.

We create wall to save ourselves from some future threats. It may happen in office, between mother-in-law and daughter-in-law and even between husband and wife because we conceive idea how other will react and start behaving. On the basis of that conception we create barriers for securing future insecurities.

First we should accept and identify barriers and then think that they are created by me only and I can only remove them. Wherever we feel void in relationship we should give a pause and think. It can be only because of the above three reasons and we should identify them and be aware to remove them.

One may be having perception of right different than the other person who has recently joined the family. Persons have habits since long being tradition of their family. They develop a belief system that this is a right habit and there can be no other option. They feel anything other than their habit cannot be correct. The other person may be having different habit and from their point of view that may be absolutely right. In such situations both may think each other's habit wrong. If in such situation one wants to tell other that his habit is right and must be followed by the other this is a feeling of control and causes conflict.

People's habits and Sanskars can be different from ours. We can see only through the filter of our Sanskar and we feel our perspective is right. For others, what is right for us may not be right to them. They are different from us; not wrong.

Conflicts are more internally than externally. In order to be a successful person in profession, business, community service, politics or any field of life the first requisite is to be a good human being with clarity of mind. We have to have open heart to accept, love and appreciate everybody, whosoever, comes in our contact. Spiritualism teaches us to be a better human being, keep the mind open and silent and tells us about our originality which is truthfulness, love everybody and be positive in life. It develops confidence and makes you feel all the time that you are a nice person full of love and compassion for everybody.

If we are in conflict with someone we need to heal the relationship. We need to send them vibrations of compassion, love and good wishes. To send good wishes we should not create a single negative thought about them. When we think that they have wronged us, we create negative thoughts of anger, hurt or hatred. Then the wishes which are travelling from us to them are not good wishes. To create the right vibrations we have to convince ourselves that they had a reason for whatever they did.

We understand that they did what they did because they were emotionally disturbed and not connected to their true self. We accept that they were not themselves, they were unwell. Then hatred changes to compassion. In the face of any conflict or exploitation we need to be calm and stable inside and yet take action outside. Whatever is happening is a return of our past Karmik account, and our stability now helps to settle the account.

Our thoughts create our destiny. Even if some external factors are unfavorable, even if people around us are not sending the right energy, if we create the right thought energy, things will go right. If people around us have belief systems which we do not agree, we should respect their beliefs system. We should not ridicule them. They are weak and our rejection makes them weaker. Let us respect them, empower them and gradually help them to experiment a new way of living. Respect to each other is the binding force in a relationship. Love, respect and trust are emotions of a person; they should not be dependent on others. We should not expect them in return.

The most common mistake in relationship is disrespect. We do not accept if somebody is not respecting as we wish; may be because of his some personal reasons. Sometimes we may also not be respecting the other person because of some of our own reasons. Giving respect means fully accepting others without even criticizing in the mind.

"When we respect life, we won't destroy life.
When we respect life, we won't exploit life.
When we respect life, we won't hurt life.
When we respect life, we won't judge life.
When we respect life, we cannot but love all of life."
BY: Manal Ghosain

When we judge someone we do not define them, we are defining ourselves. We perceive others only through the filter of our Sanskars. So when we define them we are actually defining our filter, which is our Sanskars. Different people will create a different image about one individual depending on their own Sanskars. Let us focus our attention on people's qualities, while creating an image of them in our mind. So whenever we are in conflict, we have to be aware that whether we are damaging the relationship or healing it .It is our attitude which will decide the people for whom we create beautiful thoughts, our relationship with them will be in harmony. Even if we do not approve of someone's behaviour, let us not criticize them in our mind. Even if our Sanskars do not match we can still be in harmony with them only by taking care that we are not thinking negative about them.

My love with me is a gift, I expect nothing in return. What you do with this gift is up to you. No matter what happens, I take each opportunity to decide who I am in spite of you, rather than finding out to who I am in response to you. I prefer to grow in love rather than shrinking in response. Keep sharing with yourself. Let not any body's response affect our original quality of love. I know myself, being full of love and peaceful soul. It is in spite of others, so it is not affected by other's reactions.

I will like to share with you my very personal story which changed my life.

"Sometimes incidents happen, in spite of your trying best to avoid them. The situations are created; relationships are dented and things take a shape which you never wanted. This is known as past Karmic account. But our present good Karmas can give you another opportunity to come out of that situation and change the relationships as you wanted them to be. But it becomes our choice at that time to avail that opportunity or lose it going into the past reasons. I have to narrate that once in my life it so happened that because of some reasons my terms with my eldest son got strained. The things took bad shape and we had to ultimately get separated and our relationship and talking terms came to a standstill. After sometime one day I received a call from my son that he is feeling very unhappy about all which has happened and wants to come back. By God's grace instantly good sense prevailed and I replied it is very good. This is what we all wanted that we should all remain united. So let us avail this and from that day we are having same love and affection".

Points to ponder

- We should take care of our relationships for our happiness. We should not be guided by the short term benefits from our relationships. We should be prepared to do the required sacrifice to maintain the relationship.

- Relationship is not a give and take relationship. Don't just behave as others behave with you, but behave in a way which you expect from others to behave with you. We should not talk to others in such a way in which we don't want others to talk to us.

- Best relationship is not the one which brings together the perfect people. Relationship requires each individual to learn to live with imperfection of others. One should learn to admire other person's values and qualities.

- Relationship based on love and respect has a spark which can never be extinguished. Very small gesture of love may bring back even more love. Be aware don't say or do any such thing which may kill the spark. Be first to take first step of that gesture or imitative which may ignite that spark of love. Don't wait for other to take that step.

- Trust is the greatest binding force in the relationship. Normally trust comes very late and it is first thing to go. Whereas, it should be the basis of relationship and should be the last thing to go.

- We many a times develop the habit of doubting and find it difficult to trust even family members, friends and other relations. Instead of doubting we should communicate and feel that I wished them to behave differently, forget and forgive but don't stop talking.

- When computer is hung, CTRL+ALT+DEL, similarly when life is hung, when your close relationship is strained; control, alter and delete your negativity. Create positive thoughts for each other and you will see that the relationship will again start flowing with love and happiness.

- Creation of thought that someone is wrong as per our perception means we are disrespecting him. Understanding that they are different means we respect them and their perspective.

- The best way to resolve the conflict is to remove the hurt and pain created by ourselves which is creating obstacles in accepting the other person. We should resolve our internal conflict and should start appreciating the other person.

- We should not put labels on people and start seeing them though that label. By putting label we will always radiate negative energy to them and receive the same from them. When we go beyond labels and give love and respect as a soul to soul connection it will heal ourselves and cool other also.

HURT AND STRESS THERAPY

Quote from unknown author

"Ships don't sink because of water around them. Ships sink because of the water that gets in them. Don't let what's happening around you get inside you and weigh you down".

From "Happiness in a Nutshell" by Andrew Matthews

"You get motivated by doing things, not thinking about them"

"Next time you are upset, remember it's not so much people who make you angry, as your thoughts about them"

"Whatever thoughts are causing you pain, they are only thoughts. You can change a thought" "Where did we get the idea that if we don't forgive people, they suffer?"

"The only way to beat fear is to face it"

"If we are honest with ourselves, we can list almost everything that's ever happened to us - and see how we helped create it"

"The happiest people don't worry too much about whether life is fair or not. They just get on with it"

"If you want peace of mind, stop labeling everything that happens as good or bad"

"You give your best not because you need to impress people. You give your best because that's the only way to enjoy your work"

"When life is sweet and that little voice says: It can't last! Tell yourself: Maybe it's about to get better!"

"Loving people means giving them freedom to be who they choose to be and where they choose to be. Love is allowing people to be in your life out of choice"

One gets stressful only because one does not know how to manage this body. We have become owner of this wonderful mechanism of body without knowing how to manage it or use it. We are managing it accidentally. Every machine with the least friction works more efficiently and last long. Our body is wonderful mechanism. By mechanism means, it can work systematically. Everyone carries the same mechanism but there is difference between people to people. Basically we are happy BEING. We are happy when we are child and so we should be happier when we grow. We have wonderful unparallel body mechanism but we don't have user's manual. We have to learn it and not run it accidentally. To be peaceful and happy is our fundamental requirement. We are capable of being peaceful and happy but we are searching that from **DIVINE**.

Our every thought, word and action is our creation. Situations come to us from outside but our responses are completely our choice. People may cheat, betray, trouble me but the emotions I create are my responsibility. I create my emotional wounds and I need to heal myself. If I say I cannot change my habits, then I am giving myself a negative affirmation and writing a destiny of pain.

Past incidents are triggers which we use to create thoughts now. We have a choice how much pain we create and how long. Never be harsh or critical with yourself or compare with others. Acceptance and love is the first step to healing. Don't leave emotional wounds to be healed with time. We become weaker and vulnerable to more wounds. Resolve the issue and heal the wound.

People see us through the filter of their Sanskar. It's like the colour of glasses they are wearing, they can see us only in that colour. This may not be the truth. If we know our qualities and weakness then we are not dependant on others to know about our self. We should know where we were, where we are and where we want to go on our journey of transformation. No comparison with others.

Like others see us through the filter of their Sanskars we also see our self through the labels we put on our self and through our acquired Sanskars. Our name, degree profession, position are labels that we put on our identity. We use these labels to answer the question 'Who am I'. Ego is attachment to a wrong image of self. My body, my name, my family, my degree, everything that was mine, we called it 'I' and we forgot the real 'I'. We create an image of who we are and then get attached to that image. When someone says something about the image we get hurt.

Detachment means awareness that I am separate from the body, role and responsibility. We then see things in the right perspective, take accurate decisions and not suffer pain. Let us be aware – I the soul am playing the role of parent, spouse and professional. Whatever may be the role, the personality of I the actor, a personality of peace, love and wisdom should reflect in every role. I am a soul and I am interacting with other souls playing different roles.

"Detachment is not giving up the things in this world, but accepting the fact and to be continuously aware that nothing is permanent."

Zen Meditation Practitioner Aditya Ajmera

Daily study of spiritual knowledge changes our consciousness from the illusion that I am the body and role, to the truth, I am a soul. As it is the consciousness, so are the thoughts and behaviour. When the consciousness is I am a body, then happiness is looked for in material things. When the consciousness I am a soul, then happiness is to be given because it is who I am.

Sanskars get created after a particular thought is brought into action repeatedly. Meditation is the process of silencing the conscious mind and creating a pure and powerful thought. This thought will get planted like a powerful seed in the subconscious mind. Then pay attention to bring thought into practice during the day. So that it leaves an imprint. Done repeatedly it will become a Sanskar. When in our interacting we are using the original sanskars of the spirit, the soul, we are spiritual.

My every thought is followed by a feeling. Feelings over a period of time develop my attitude. Attitude comes into action. Action done repeatedly becomes a habit. All my habits put together is my personality. At every step in life this personality determines my destiny. The sanskars of my thought is my belief systems, information and past experiences. If God writes our destiny then he being a perfect being and our parent he would write a perfect destiny. He will not be biased and write better for one child than the others.

We have to be aware all the time that we don't create stress for ourselves and others. We have to empower us and others by appreciation. We have a strong belief system that unless we create pressure and competitiveness we can't give our best. Similarly, we think of others also working for us. As long as this pressure and competitiveness, makes you more determined to achieve your targets it is good, but the moment it gets to a level, where fear of failure enters in your thought and we develop a feeling, how we will be able to do it, or what will happen if I fail to achieve; it becomes stress. The stress becomes fear. We want to create same stress or fear in the minds of people working with us. So in order to get best out of them we try to motivate them, using this stress or fear as tool. In this whole process we forget that fear or stress is a negative energy and the result motivation, which we are seeking, is a positive energy. We should think how a negative energy can generate positive energy. So for creation of motivation, the positive energy is required with love, compassion, appreciation and support system. Negative energy will never bring positive energy, we may only temporarily see that it is worthy and working for you but it can never bring results.

Criticism is always disempowerment. In case, you want to give your feedback, you just need not to say that your work is perfect, if it is not, you have to give critical energy. There is a great difference between criticism with negative thinking and giving critical energy. The words don't matter, the intention behind those words matter. You can empower someone while giving the feedback by appreciating saying yes, it is good, but you can dis empower people, if your intention is not good. So it is the intention with which you are giving critical energy to another person that matters and can bring best out of yourself and others. Our intention should be that we want ourselves and others to keep excelling in their work. We should be aware, who the worker is; worker is energy and we have to empower the energy. In fact, it is the energy of the worker which works. We should have trust in ourselves and others and we have to facilitate, guide and empower to get best out of ourselves and others.

There is also another belief system that if we appreciate or show leniency towards people working with us, they will come on our head. Instead of that if we just think that how I will like my seniors, if any, if none then just imagine, would have behaved to get me motivated. How can they get best out of me, how I would want them to speak to me? I may be senior now, but when I was child or junior, how was I expecting my parents to talk to me. I should think whether my personality is such that if my parents would have spoken nicely to me, I would have taken undue advantage of it. It is in our hand to create work culture..

It is very clear that fear and stress can never enhance performance; it will always damage the performance. Now think if we change the environment and work culture then what will happen. We start appreciating giving feedback in the right perceptive; entire staff will begin to feel full energy of love, acceptance and support. They will themselves work and will be having a feeling of belongingness to the work and will come for work with their heart with mind. There will be so much transparency that if anyone makes a mistake, he will own it up himself, because he has no fear and knows you are there not for scolding but for guidance. They will not hide their mistakes and stop blaming others or something else for it. You will know the mistake and deficiencies to make them good immediately.

I will like to share my one personal experience with you. I lost my wife in 2006 and after sometimes I developed the emotion of getting hurt more frequently. As you all know, what wife can do for her husband, one cannot get from anybody else. We are sometimes not able to change our expectations and start expecting those things from our children. I had developed a belief system that I am getting more hurt now because formerly I was able to share my feelings with wife and she used to pacify and I used to be alright. One day I thought, since she is not there why I can't share now with me. The time I got this awareness and came out of that thinking my hurt was reduced considerably and then I strengthen myself further more and decided that now I will not give permission myself to get hurt by anybody. Believe me it has brought miraculous change and now I don't get hurt; let anybody behave in any way. I surrendered my hurt to my Guruji Shree Ramesh Ji and now the moment I Just have any feeling of hurt, my Guru Comes in front of me as a shield

Normally, we feel that now we have become busier and we don't get enough time to complete our work. It is not that we have started working more and have become busy but it is the distances, traffic and all other sorts of things going around us that we are left with less time to complete more work. So we create tension of it for which nothing is in our hands than just to plan our things better. But we have made it routine to accept these small pressures and allow them to be converted into tension or stress. We have accepted it as a normal life and are living with these stresses as natural. It becomes a part of our life and for everybody around us. We have to think over it and see whether it is a right belief system.

Our belief system of accepting small stress and worries as natural and part of the game, gradually grows in number and becomes a burden which we find difficult to carry. This develops irritation and frustration which makes us further tense and unstable. So it becomes our habit to have little tension, little worried, keeping little anger all the time remain irritated. These little things go on and start affecting our health and creating physical problems or headache etc, and we start accepting them as natural. This affects quality of our life and even after having all materialistic success and enough resources we are not happy from inside and that unhappiness is reflected on our face. We stand trapped for bigger problems.

Our awareness will guide us that it is all happening because we have accepted little stress and worries as natural and have not started thinking that our stress is because of the situation and circumstance outside, which are not under my control. We think situations are the main cause of our stress. We go on accepting these little situations to continue creating little stress and worries. These situations go on growing into bigger situations creating bigger stress.

So it becomes our habit and only when big situations are created we completely focus on it to combat the situation taking it as our responsibility. This feeling was not there when we were facing situation creating little pressures and we were taking them as natural. They were creating irritation as their natural behaviour. While, the same people facing bigger situation taking it as their own responsibility to get out of it, they were able to suppress and come out of their stress. They were able to suppress their grief and were determined to cross that difficulty. They are, many a times, able also to cross that difficulty. But in this whole process they find themselves completely broken.

Our awareness can make us strong enough to break this cycle and give strength to avoid this. To avoid stress we should start trying little things. First we should start to cross it with stability. We somehow, think that stress is an ailment beyond us. It depends upon lots of circumstances, situations and people. No doubt, it is like ailment but not physical; first we should start believing that it can be cured by me and me alone. The moment we feel little disturbed we should be aware of it. Every morning we should check the pulse of our thought and check the beats of our thoughts whether they are natural or fast or too fast and if we find that some thoughts are running fast and that of a negative quality we should fix them at this level itself.

We should be conscious that even little stress affects our performance, our memory power, and decision making capacity. It also creates confusion anger, resentment, painful thoughts which affect the heart and other vital parts of the body. We should just not think of postponing our stress by taking break or holiday. We have just to give rest to the mind. We are required to give mind a rest for just a few minutes every day. We should take breaks or holidays but not for postponing our stress but to fill us with more enjoyment and to get more time for our family and ourselves.

We should keep a constant watch on our mind, how it is working, what quality of thoughts it is generating. The solution of stress is in our way of thinking and the moment we start enjoying our work, our situations our studies and our normal routine we start having holiday and break every day.

Stress is ultimately my fearful thought, stress is my worry. We should be aware that stress does not depend on pressures but it is the outcome of our inner weakness. So we have to increase our inner strength.

We need to have one paradigm shift in our belief system that stress is my creation; it is not created by a situation or a person. I alone create it even if nothing is happening outside. I can actually create it. As soon as we point a finger at others for creation of it we outflow our energy; we disempower ourselves so we have to strengthen ourselves only and have to take full control of our mind and move forward towards stability and think of present moment only.

We have become very much health conscience and take care to detoxify our bodies by going on a special diet etc, but we do not think to detoxify our mind. We have not to do much to detoxify our mind. Simply everyday sit down calmly for some time just 5-10 minutes and think the past is over and done with; may be the other person acted wrongly; that's alright but actually who created hurt and who is still creating the hurt. The event took place years ago but I am still creating hurt about the same. How long I am going to keep this on my mind. I have to stop this and change till I end the bitterness. I will not be happy unless I forgive and forget not for others but for myself.

Targets, pressures, deadlines, exams are natural but stress is our choice. Stress is equal to pressures (Situations) divided by resilience (Inner Strength). My first responsibility in any situation is to first take charge of my state of mind because that is the only thing which is in my control.

Every day we should remember I will remain peaceful irrespective of whatever happens. Anger will not come, whoever, I will meet I will look at their qualities not their weaknesses. I will not criticize any one. I am powerful; I can do whatever I decide to do. Our thought is the seed which result in our feeling and our expression to the outer world. So, if our thoughts are filled with negativity and fear then automatically everything around us will also result in same negativity. To come out of this, one need to work on him. We have to spend some time with the self and process the reason which has created the problem.

A silent mind is one which is positive. Negative thoughts are too many in number and therefore create confusion and then even if the solution is clearly in front of us we will not be able to see. When we develop the habit of positive thoughts then only a right kind of thought will emerge and taking decision will become easy. When the mind is silent we don't have to think very logically, the right solution emerges from the intuition and it is a solution which we could have never thought logically. Positive thinking is developed with constant attention and practice. Throughout the day a stop in between for few minutes and watching what is going on our mind; if it is not the right kind of thought stop and change it; start talking to your mind generally; Calm it and it will listen to you. Whenever any unnecessary or waste thought comes tell your mind that is not useful for you or for your relationship and change it. Try and look at your mind for at least one minute in every hour. In the morning when you begin the day sit in silence for 5 minutes and program your mind with positive thoughts.

Even after doing everything above written, in spite of our best efforts, we feel still hurt, then I feel instead of avoiding the situation we should communicate to the people the reason which we are not able to adjust and are getting hurt. This we should do with positive thinking and love, thinking that the other person will also be thoughtful of not creating the situation again. It will make us light and will help us to meet our object of keeping relationship intact.

The Secret of success is not in being stressful but to remain calm and happy all the time 24/7. PRATICE, PRATICE and PRATICE only can make that possible.

Points to ponder

- We create pressure and competitiveness thinking we can get best out of ourselves and others by creating it. It is good as long as it is making us more determined to achieve our target without fear of failure.
- Criticism is always disempowerment. We should give feedback with critical energy but with the intention to see that they excel in their work.
- We should not hesitate to appreciate people thinking that appreciation will reach to their head and their

expectations from us will increase .It is in our hands to create work culture around us.

- We should start appreciating; giving feedback in the right perspective to entire staff and everybody around us with full energy of love, acceptance and support. They will have a feeling of belongingness and will come for work with their heart and mind.

- Sometimes hurt and insult inflicted upon us creates a feeling of guilt. We forget our originality and carry that hurt thinking time will heal the wound. Treat this as mistake and separate it from yourself.

- Many a times we create stress and tension for the situations which are not in our hand. These small stresses and pressures gradually grow in number and become a burden. So, it becomes our habit to remain little tense, little worried, little angry, irritated and frustrated all the time.

- When big situations are created we completely focus on them to combat the situation taking it as our responsibility and most of the times get out of them also. So it is in our hand but this feeling of responsibility is not there when we are creating stress and tension because of small things.

- Take breaks and holidays, not for postponing your stress but to fill yourself with more enjoyment and to get more time for your family and yourself.

- Many a times we hold external reasons responsible for our stress. We go in denial mode and feel ourselves helpless in not creating stress. We have to believe strongly that no one, no situation and nothing is cause of my stress it is created by me and I can stop them, change them or increase them

KNOW
YOUR EMOTIONS

<u>Quote from Sadhguru Jaggi Vasudev</u>

"Joy is a natural phenomenon. Misery is your creation. Whatever may come our way, how we respond to it and what we make out of it is 100% ours. Be the light of your life. When you just look at the long term span of this creation you are just a tiny happening. But you think too much of yourself that is the biggest problem".

Human beings are full of emotions. They are very visible and evident. They are our biggest strength and sometimes they become our biggest weakness also. We have to understand that if we detach ourselves from our body and think of 'I' as being; we are pure emotionless with only one emotion of love for the whole universe. We have the power to control our emotions by mind which is under our control and let us flow love only as our original emotion.

We create emotions in every thought and we generate 25-30 thoughts every minute. We have all sorts of good and bad emotions. Like - Anger, Jealousy, Hatred, Greed, attachment, Ego, Sex, Guilt, etc. They are created out of our thinking process. They are not the original emotions. The original emotions are -Love, Truth, Service, Compassion, and Purity.

As a matter of fact one has not to do anything to be happy only he has not to do anything which may reduce his happiness. We have not to work to increase our happiness but we should work to see that it is not depleted. When anybody is jealous of you, create compassion for him as he is sick. When you don't get success take responsibility and move on.

Our every thought or emotion created by us influences others. How we feel, the thoughts come into the words and actions; it becomes our experience and this gets recorded and impressions are created on the Soul. These become our vibrations. What we speak is first created as thoughts. The thoughts could have been created earlier and stirred. When we use the phrase, "Slip of tongue or we didn't mean it", it only means we felt it earlier but had then decided not to speak it.

"Unexamined thoughts, habits or action may offer some deceptive gain or pleasure but eventually it takes away something most valuable from our life, which we have ever wished for."

Zen Meditation Practitioner Aditya Ajmera

When in response to a situation or behaviour we create certain emotions and hold them, then those emotions are stored in the memory. These emotions will replay on our mind many times and cause pain and then also come in words. Let us counsel our mind understand the person and then store the scene with acceptance. Any negative emotion hurt, resentment, rejection or any painful emotion created and held in mind will become part of our personality. The pain becomes a part of our energy field and starts coming into other healthy relationships.

We should be aware all the time that we are born as actors and whatever we are doing acting as per direction of our mind. Like when we perform in a drama our focus is on our performance and our script, not dependent on the performance of co-actors or situations, and circumstances. Even, if situations or circumstances are not favourable or the co-actor does not perform well, forgets his lines we will keep performing well and even help the co-actors to bring them back on track.

We have to keep attention on our performance in every scene of life. The criteria that we have crossed the scene well are that we are at ease, the mind is feeling nice, body is relaxed and co-actors in the scene are feeling nice. People respect and feel nice with us not because what we have acquired in our life but because of what we have radiated to them. If we are humble and radiate love, kindness and compassion it will make us and people around us feel nice.

Like we take care when we get a photograph clicked, we need to take care of our every thought, word and action getting recorded on the soul. There is no retake on the recording and it is an external recording which will always remain on the soul and will go with us in the next birth. So, we should be very careful and watch our thoughts at every moment. Thoughts of all sorts may come but we have to erase them before they are recorded and get converted into words and actions.

Emotions are our creation. We should take full responsibility of creating emotions. When we try to control our emotions they remain inside and we want to communicate it to vent it out, but if whenever we get emotional and take the responsibility of not creating that emotion, we will not create the emotion and will not need to communicate it and vent it out.

Like we take care of what we speak to others, we need to be careful of how we speak to ourselves. We are constantly listening to our inner conversation. When we think or speak negatively to another person, the extent to which they get affected is their choice. But we will not be able to stop the negative energy from affecting our own mind and body.

Even if our thoughts are negative, let us first stop reacting in words and actions and then practice to stop generation of negative thoughts. Whenever any thought comes to create emotion we can control our reaction in words and actions, but instead of controlling the emotion, we should not allow it to be created. We should take full responsibility of its creation. Then we will be able to stop its creation.

About a hundred years ago, a man looked at the morning newspaper and to his utter surprise and horror, read his name in the obituary column. The newspapers had reported the death of the wrong person by mistake.

His first response was shock. Am I here or there? When he regained his composure, his second thought was to find out what people had said about him.

The obituary read, "Dynamite King Dies." And also "He was the merchant of death." This man was the inventor of dynamite and when he read the words "merchant of death," he asked himself a question, "Is this how I am going to be remembered?" He got in touch with his feelings and decided that this was not the way he wanted to be remembered. From that day onward, he started working towards peace. His name was Alfred Nobel and he is remembered today by the great Nobel Prize.

Alfred Nobel got in touch with his feelings and redefined his values.

What is my legacy?

How would I like to be remembered?
Will I be spoken well of?
Will I be remembered with love and respect?
Will I be missed?

Let us now deal with various emotions individually Emotions like – Guilt, Jealousy, Anger, Irritation, Greed, Sex, attachment, are very strong. We also have positive emotions like love, compassion, truth, service and purity. These are our original emotions. We have to train our mind to know beforehand when we are getting negative emotions. When we will start recognizing the thoughts which create these negative emotions, we will be able to stop their creation. So they will not be recorded on our mind and will never come in our words or actions. We will never criticize others for creation of those emotions. We must understand nobody else can create emotions in us, it is only we and our thoughts who the creator of these emotions. We will be able to handle these negative emotions with love and test them with truth and purity.

Guilt –

Guilt is a very powerful emotion. Sometimes when we feel from inside that we have done something wrong and as its consequences others whom we love are pained or disturbed, we develop emotion of guilt. We feel I have been disturbed I have lost my happiness, but I can bear it as the mistake was committed by me but why others, whom I don't want to give pain, should suffer. I am having constant pain that I am the cause of other's suffering, they all are feeling me responsible for their pain but are not saying anything. They love me so much that they don't want to increase my pain but they are all in their mind holding me responsible. In such situation we don't garner courage to accept that this all has happened because of me. I will handle it successfully and I can reduce my pain by just thinking that it **happened cannot be undone and** I will come out of it and will not make myself unhappy any more. If we can gather such courage in ourselves and start feeling like that also we can come out of our guilt and see its effect on others around us. But we normally have the belief system that it is not possible for me to come out of this guilt and time will heal it automatically. So, we leave our wound open to heal and that also on time. We are not taking any care to heal the wound. We are trying to distract our mind from that by engaging in other activities.

It takes long time and in between we are bearing the pain and are developing negativity and fear also. We have to shift our belief system and take the courage to face the situation thinking that done is done but why should it pain me anymore. I will take care of my wound and be healthy and happy. Your this determination will bring you out of your emotion of guilt and every person around you will forget it very soon and will be more positive and confident of dealing with the situation.

While, taking responsibility of the guilt and accepting that I have to get rid of this we may revisit the whole incident and think whether it was a wrong decision or I have messed it up somewhere because of conflict of egos and lack of understanding. It is quite possible that we may find out the solution and the decision which we were feeling as guilt may change into the blessing. We should always remember that we take various decisions to make ourselves happy but because of many reasons, self created, those decisions change into making us sad and unhappy leading us to feel it as guilt.

Guilt is created sometimes when we have not listened to our conscious and done something which was not in agreement with our conscious and then in future if we get some adverse results we may develop guilt that I am a bad person and lower our self esteem. We weaken ourselves and lose strength. The person has to gather strength by thinking that I made a mistake out of my ego. I am not a bad person, because I am a pure soul and nice person. I committed mistake and will not do it again. In this way one can remove his guilt and be ready to come out of that guilt. In having guilt one is simply wasting time, creating pain, depleting strength. Accept the mistake, feel sorry about that, leave the ego and commit not to do it again.

JEALOUSY:

Jealousy is a feeling rather than emotion. It is felt, only when we make comparisons. It is widely felt that we do not develop the feeling of jealousy with the people, with whom we don't compare ourselves. As people who are less privileged than us we do not compare ourselves with them and so we don't develop a feeling of jealousy with them. Similarly, we also don't develop feeling of jealousy with the people who are much more privileged than us and we do not feel that we can in any way compare ourselves with them. So it is very clear that this feeling of jealousy comes out of our Sanskar of comparison. The instinct of comparison arises from the feeling that, whatever, we are today is the outcome of our own Sanskars and work. So we think how we got less and somebody else got more. If we think, there is no basis of such thinking. We have to be aware that whatever we get is not the outcome of only our present efforts. Our past Sanskars, our family Sanskars and our own experiences and Sanskars created out of our actions are responsible for everything we get. So everybody has his own past Sanskars, family Sanskars and his own experiences, and accordingly he gets the results. Thus, actually there can be no comparison.

Furthermore, if we just trust the principle that whatever, we have achieved is not our own achievement but there are lots of other forces, which when get together bring the results. We will be always satisfied with ourselves and never feel jealous of any body. We will also change our Sanskar of comparing with others.

Jealousy is not the feeling of competing with anybody; when you are competing with anybody you are actually not jealous but you are trying to improve yourself to compete with him. Feeling of competition brings best out of you and you have very positive feeling, whereas, jealousy does not motivate you to improve yourself but it gives negative feeling of making the other down to surpass them. It leads to negative thoughts and inspire you to adopt any means to surpass the other. Jealousy also brings a feeling of inferiority in you because you are not preparing yourself to compete with the other person about whom you are jealous. This feeling of inferiority depletes your strength further and you start feeling depressed. Your spirit and excitement to do better and better is dampened.

To control the feeling of jealousy the best way is to be aware that whatever God has given to us or whatever we have is all God given and if we regularly pay our gratitude to God then we will feel satisfied and contented and will not have the feeling of jealousy. We should always think that if somebody is having more than me it is because God has bestowed upon him, so if God has bestowed more upon him then we should also respect him as God has respected him by bestowing more, so we should have no reason to be jealous.

ANGER-

Anger is an addiction. We find it quite hard to leave any addiction. We have to be aware that when we become angry first we create negative energy within us. Then we should realize that my anger on somebody will affect him and his family. That negative feeling will also come back to us.

We have the power to control anger but we sometimes use this power and sometimes we don't use this power. We have the power to be peaceful but when some other person shows anger we forget our power and we are overpowered by them.

IRRITATION:

We create irritation when someone is doing something again and again which according to us is not correct. The thing is being repeated again and again, in spite of my objecting to it many times, we are getting disturbed. If we accept that we are getting disturbed by that act and not by the person we may not create irritation. If we create feeling of non-acceptance of that act and the person who is doing it we create irritation. If a child does something we normally don't get irritated but if a person on whom we feel we have control does the same thing we get irritated. We can avoid it by being aware.

Many a times, we make ourselves dependent upon others to take care of our emotions. Sometimes we feel hurt and then take the help of somebody to vent out our hurt and then with his help get over the hurt. Supposing we lose that person and then our Sanskar of getting hurt increases because we are not able to vent it and get help of the other person to get over the hurt we go on increasing our sanskar to get hurt quickly and repeatedly.

We can get over it by just changing our thought that we don't need anybody outside to share our hurt or emotion we can share it with ourselves. When we will share it with ourselves we will seek reply from our consciousness that is it of any use to create hurt or that emotion. We will always get a reply that we are the master of our own and we can create our own emotions, why we should create our emotions in reaction or response to behavior or doing of others. The moment we will take control of our emotions the creation of it will seek our permission before creation. Gradually we will move to a state when we will be confident that we would not allow anybody else to hurt me or create any negative emotion. We will become masters of our own emotions. It will radiate positivity and we will see that others will also start behaving in a nice way and ultimately they will also get rid of their negativity. It will make your energy moment SATSANG and you will start enjoying every moment. We should take responsibility of creation of our emotions.

When we are in the consciousness of our position, role and relationships we expect others to behave according to the role. When we do not get what we expect we create all sorts of emotions. Let us be in our true consciousness of a soul interacting with another soul. Then we will accept the Sanskars of the other soul and will radiate our original

To apologies to someone means to send very powerful loving energy to heal them and a determined thought to do right next time. We cannot have a single negative thought for them because it will add pain to their hurt.

The first step to transformation is not to justify your negative emotion but to take personal responsibility of having created it. When we justify our emotion we blame others for it. We then expect them to change and do not find the need to change ourselves. To change any habit we need to answer three questions. Why should I change? How do I change? And most important Do I want to change? Unless want to change is there, how to change will not get implemented.

We have to resolve the issues on the mind before sleeping. Give answers to the disturbed mind or give instructions that we will think about this tomorrow. Silence the mind, else the body will sleep mind will keep thinking and not get changed.

If we allow situation to overpower the mind we start depleting our power. Rise above the situation. Focus on the solution rather than thinking about why the problem happened. Think about the solution not the problem. Till we keep thinking about the past which is not in our control we are wasting time and energy.

Many a times we are aware but we think that if every time we will be aware of it how we will do our other responsibilities. So we have to fix priority. If a woman carrying a child with earthen pot on the head she will take care of child more than the earthen pot on head. So it is the question of priority. So we have to control our mind on priority basis.

The mind is like a child. Take care of your child and also all your responsibilities like family, career and health. The first priority will be the child within and then everything outside. While taking care of your responsibilities the child might start crying, the mind starts getting irritated, angry or hurt; withdraw for a minute from activity and heal the child, talk to the mind and change the quality of thoughts.

The child within is not in our control. No one taught us what to think or how much to think. Discipline this child with the love not force or harshness. While dealing with others remember we are dealing with the child within them. Responsibility means the ability to respond the right way in every situation. So the priority list of the responsibilities will be self, family and work. It will take care of our emotional well being. we will have good relations and then perform well at work.

If we are carrying some problem with somebody and we want explanation from them, believing from inside that their explanation will also not satisfy us, will not work. We should first resolve inside. We have to think how long we want to carry this hurt with us. So we have to decide and resolve. We many a time resolve other's problems and expect others to resolve our problems but we don't try to resolve our problems ourselves.

Like we choose the clothes we wear let us choose the thoughts we create. We should choose the thoughts which suit our personality which are comfortable to us and which will be appreciated by others. We create 25000 to 30000 thoughts in a day. Our thoughts become our energy field. Our energy field moves with us and radiates to everyone like the perfume we use.

Even if we create hurt, resolve the issue and reduce the time for which we will remain in pain. Else we can carry it for months and years. Answer the mind and close the topic, heal the pain.

Our every thought is followed by a feeling. Feelings over a period of time develop our attitude. Attitude comes out into action. Any action done repeatedly becomes a habit. All our habits put together is our personality. Our personality creates our destiny.

Points to ponder

- We generate 25-30 thoughts every minute and our thoughts create emotions. Negative emotions created are held in mind and become part of our personality.
- We are born actors and mind is our director. We must take charge of the mind. Thoughts of all sorts may come but we have the power to erase them before they get recorded and get converted into words and actions.

- Emotions are our creation. We should take full responsibility of their creation. Blaming people, situation or the past or the world is the prime reason of depletion of our soul power

- Guilt is a very powerful emotion. We can remove it just by thinking that happened cannot be undone. We should not leave it on time to subside. We should accept and take responsibility and decide that I will not do it again.

- Jealousy comes out of comparison. Don't compare and be contented with whatever we have got. Everybody gets according to this own present and past actions.

- We should not justify our negative emotions but should take personal responsibility of having created it. We think why and how we should change our emotion. But for transformation we will have to decide that we want to change this.

- Even if we create hurt, resolve the issue and reduce the time for which we will remain in pain. Our every thought creates feeling which develops our attitude which creates our habits and gets converted in our personality and destiny.

- Anger and irritation can be avoided by being aware that we have the power to control it and we will not allow others to overpower our mind. The energy of love is our natural quality. It gets blocked when we become judgmental about people.

LEAD AN
ENRICHING LIFE

Quote from Swami Vivekananda

"Stand Up, Be Bold, Be Strong. Take the whole responsibility on your own shoulders and know that you are the creator of your own destiny".

Quote from G.I Gurdjieff

"I ASK YOU TO BELIEVE NOTHING that you cannot verify for yourself."

We are born with last so many Janmas SANSKARS. We have carried forward those SANSKARS. We can very well understand it by noticing different children have different habits. Some are weeping frequently. Some are always smiling. Some like some toys and others like different toys. So we have all come with different SANSKARS. These SANSKARS guide us to form our habits. We start taking them as natural, as they have come from our childhood. If somebody points out some weakness in us we feel, yes I have this weakness but it is there with me from childhood, so I can't do anything about it.

We are a powerful soul and carrying Sanskars with us. Some Sanskars are of our past lives, some we have acquired from family and some have been acquired by us by our experiences of life through many situations in life. But we have original Sanskars of our soul - Love, Truth, Happiness, Purity, Bliss and Power.

So, the process of empowerment of soul means to remove the dirt of other Sanskar and bring back our **BEING** to its original Sanskars. We have to make ourselves strong enough to see that external factors do not affect our inner strength. When we allow external factors to affect our original state of being our emotional health physical health, relationships, and quality of sleep and overall our qualities of life get affected. Our vibrations of anxiety radiates around us and influence everybody, whosoever, comes in contact.

When we adopt a particular way to respond to a particular type of situation it creates certain groove on our mind and it becomes our Sanskar and we start responding in the same way to the situations. We can consciously understand it and start responding differently and create a new groove in our mind. We will see the change. This thing can be understood by observing others. People respond differently in different situations.

We normally justify our negative thoughts by blaming the situations and people around us. We have to understand that every time we justify our negative reactions by blaming other people and situations, we are disempowering ourselves. It depletes our soul power and by blaming others we are losing our power furthermore.

We have to take personal responsibility of our reactions irrespective of situation and have to empower ourselves. By doing that we are reminding ourselves that we are a powerful soul. No matter, if we have failed this time but next time we will respond differently and take charge of us. This feeling will empower our soul and prepare ourselves to face the similar situation in future strongly.

We should always remember that the purpose of our life is not in doing but in the **BEING**. The purpose of being is to feel and radiate always our original qualities of Soul- Love,

Purity, Bliss and Power in everything, whatever, we are doing.

Life is not just about acquiring and acquiring only. Some achievements are goals of life but it is not the purpose of life. Even after acquiring lots and achieving various goals it is not necessary that we will stop there and wouldn't move then furthermore. In this process of acquiring more and more, we develop a sense of fear of losing it. We develop attachment for these acquisitions which we are not able to distribute to others.

We can empower ourselves by meditating everyday to develop direct connection between us and the soul and God, the highest power. When there is an accurate connection, me the soul will get charged by God's power. While, meditating we should concentrate. Concentration means mind and intellect are together on the same subject. Mind creates the thoughts and intellect visualizes it, creating an experience for the soul.

We have to play various roles in life and we have to manage them with full responsibility. Self management means being conscious of our roles we are performing. For every event in life we normally base our action on others and situations. So we think that our roles are fixed and that is our destiny. My response, my way of talking is all dependent on others and situations. So there is somebody else who is the director and creator. We have to shift from this belief system and think that whatever we are doing we are creating as our reaction. God does not guide us to behave in a particular way.

So instead of acting as an actor we have to be creator and direct ourselves to respond. If we are aware of it all the time we will be creating our scenes and will create our own roles. So it will become interesting and will not be automated. We all know we should live in present. It is possible only when we are working with awareness. If we are walking in an automated way we will not know the present and will remain in past or future. But if we are walking with awareness we will have to think and have to be creative with awareness on every step then we will remain in present only and our thoughts will not go to past or future. If we are creative we will not feel fatigue and get engrossed in present. We have not to play thinking somebody has written our role and somebody is directing us and we are simply acting. This automated mode makes life boring. We have to be creative to remain excited every day. In every response we should think of creating better and better.

We become very serious about our position and status so we lose fun of it. We are always acting according to our position and status whereas our role is not defined by the position. Our role is to be creative in performing our role. Don't always remain a father or mother to the child; try to be creative and be his friend, counselor and enjoy the company of your child.

It is also very important that what type of people we are keeping with us because we cannot be selective. The company we keep forces us either to start acting like them or leave living with them. When we become selective we have to select because of our helplessness. So, we have to accept others. So, when we get disturbed by other's behaviour then we become slaves of other's behaviour.

Accepting is not giving up. Acceptance means that you recognize and understand your current situation. Acceptance means it gives you freedom to accept something rather than remaining in denial. You may accept or resist but can't change. Sometimes we feel that by resisting we can change the things or situations but that is not going to happen, we are just reducing our strength. Resistance is not accepting the things as they are. Suppose it is raining, I am not able to go, so we are resisting. We may accept and be peaceful to wait for it.

A great Japanese warrior named Nobunaga decided to attack the enemy although he had only one-tenth the number of men the opposition commanded. He knew that he would win, but his soldiers were in doubt. On the way he stopped at a Shinto shrine and told his men: "After I visit the shrine I will toss a coin. If heads comes, we will win; if tails, we will lose. Destiny holds us in her hand."

Nobunaga entered the shrine and offered a silent prayer. He came forth and tossed a coin. Heads appeared. His soldiers were so eager to fight that they won their battle easily.

"No one can change the hand of destiny," his attendant told him after the battle.

"Indeed not," said Nobunaga, showing a coin which had been doubled, with heads facing either way.

Thought process also plays vital role in our doings. Thought is more powerful than electromagnetic energy, color or sound. Thoughts can transfer without any boundary of time space and distance. As we all know, light travels through space, by the time it reaches to us it takes lot of time and it diminishes, but thoughts have no limiting factor. Sitting here I can transmit my thoughts across the globe. As other's thoughts can empower us or disempower us, we should think that our thoughts can also be blessing or curse for others. So don't create such thoughts, which can weaken you unless somebody has thought anything negative or ill about you, you can never feel that. Unless, somebody else has created some thoughts about you, it cannot reach to you.

Situations come does not matter; how it came does not matter; but we should think that it should not come again in future. Finish them in your mind with a smile, forget and forgive from heart. We should develop a class and the ability to walk away from a bad situation with a smile on our face and forgiveness from our heart. Don't treat difficulties in the way as obstacle we should face these difficulties and pass through them. What in the way is the way?

Meditation means, what we hear or think has to be inculcated in us. Whatever, we hear or read, we have to meditate that to adopt. Meditation gives us power and then whatever we listen or read is converted into knowledge.

Our body consciousness which creates separate identity of our body and status creates EGO. Depletion of soul power makes acquired Sanskars more powerful and then they over power our inner strength and create EGO. Let God give us serenity to accept what I can't change and give courage to change what I can change. Give wisdom to differentiate what I can change and what I cannot change.

On every step in our journey of life we have to take certain decisions. For accurate decisions, before taking decision we have to evaluate its effect on present and visualize its future consequences on us. We have to make changes at thought level, feeling level and then Sanskar level. A wise man makes his own decisions and ignorant man follows public opinion. He bases his thinking what people think.

When you really take a decision, don't just wish, and when you really commit don't just try, and while taking responsibility just not hope, you will see miracles happening. Decide, commit and take full responsibility not just wish try and hope.

If our Balance sheet is having carried forward losses we try to make up that loss and make every effort to bring our Balance sheet in profit. One should pick up first his one habit about which he feels that my one habit is such which is causing trouble and hurt to others. It is giving trouble or pain to me and persons around me and is weakening my soul. You mediate that I am aware of my habit and I can change this habit. I have to leave this habit as this depletes the strength of my soul. Some situations arise and these habits come and start depleting my energy. Let us start seeing ourselves that some such situation has arisen but I am not reacting to it as per my habit. Then think whether I can change these habits. I am so powerful that I can change it. We should constantly check ourselves about our habits which are reducing our strength. Not only ours they are reducing other's strength also.

Ego is the greatest SANSKAR, which is there in us. Ego means we feel that everybody should accept what I am saying. Self respect mean, I am not disturbed if anybody is not accepting what I am saying and so it is opposite to the Ego. When we are not disturbed, if anybody do not accept what we say, is self respect .Because in ego, we have expectation and self respect is acceptance. This is the simple way of differentiating between Ego and self respect.

I wanted to be happy, peaceful and self contented but we are trying to give happiness to 'I' by acquiring more and more. We all make ourselves dependent upon these acquired things. But in this process we get attached to our position. We develop the insecurity of fear of losing these acquired things. We do not care for ourselves but we care for these acquired things. It is said, for knowing a person ,we should know how the outer situations are affecting his mind .He is remaining stable in his mind or getting affected by just a wrong shot in the game.

We should make ourselves less dependent upon the variable external factors. We should not feel perfect because of acquired things. We need to work to achieve goals of our life and take full care of the acquired but just as a TRUSTEE. , but not make acquired as your identity. IT CAN HAPPEN ONLY WHEN WE FORGET THAT I AM THE SOUL.

Whatever decision we take even on the advice of our family or friends, we have to take responsibility of our decision, then we will not deplete the strength of our soul and will not be unhappy of the decision. When family, friends or seniors give advice we follow it either because we feel it is right for us or because we want to make them happy or because we love them, respect them or fear them. Reasons can be many but we need to remember that whatever may be the reason, the decision was ours and it was a choice we made.

For every choice made there will be repercussions. After listing down all the options and the consequences of those options we choose one option. While taking the decision we need to be very clear - I am making this choice and not say - 'I am doing this because of them, I have no other choice'. If we create a Sanskar of saying that we did not have a choice, it will deplete soul power because the soul feels powerless that it cannot take its own decision. This will be the life of a victim and we will not be happy about our decisions.

When we choose and create Karma today we have also chosen the consequences of the Karma. The consequence can come to us today, after a few days, few years or few births. This consequence is our destiny which will come to us later for a Karma which we have chosen today. Everything is predestined means everything that is coming to us is a destiny that was previously decided by us based on the Karma we choose that day. When we understand and accept that every decision is our choice we will take responsibility of our Karma and the consequence of Karma. If there are any challenges we'll face them and not blame those who have advised us.

We may get hurt physically in an accident or get hurt emotionally by any person; it is our destiny because of our past Karmas. We sometimes get indications beforehand but still we are not able to avoid it. We should take it as our destiny because of our past Karmas. We should not create guilt in ourselves because of the reasons which caused that. Whatever, may happen with us we should not create the feeling of guilt but move on taking it as destiny the consequence of our last Karmas. This will make you stable and will give strength to face that; creation of guilt weakens your soul. So we have the choice to come out of the suffering which came to us as our destiny.

We cannot change the destiny because it is an effect of our previous cause, which was a wrong Karma. How we respond to the situation or relationship now, is the energy, we are creating in the present. Irrespective of how difficult our destiny maybe we can choose powerful and positive Karmas today. Our present Karma can reduce the suffering and can make a difficult past Karmik account a pleasant experience today and a beautiful destiny for the future.

Spirituality is to be practiced in daily life. We can use spirituality in our day to day work. It does not mean anything which is other than the regular life. It is a tool to be used for getting everybody bring together. It has to be used to get its results. We have not to look up to some person or compare with anybody. We have to use spirituality as way of life and we will get result as per our practice. We have to be aware of values all the time. We have to be repeating the same all the time in our mind.

In Kaliyug, Saints are souls who have started their journey of self purification but they have been on a long journey of many births and may carry a few acquired sanskars. They are making intense efforts in this birth but if we even get to see a shade of slight ego or anger, we should not get disillusioned. They are souls who are working towards reaching a stage of complete soul consciousness, but may still have some shades of body consciousness. We should be inspired by their journey or transformation; our expectations of them being perfect may disappoint us.

Our journey of self transformation is personal. Only we know - what we were, what we are now and what we want to be. We cannot compare with others or get affected by other's opinions.

When we live with the belief system that everything is happening by the will of God, then we attribute our good and bad moments both to him. We blame him for the challenges in our life and believe that he is punishing us for our sins. This leads to the belief that if we please God, he will forgive our sins and the problems in our life will fade away. This belief system disempowers us.

God, the ocean of knowledge gives us the knowledge of right Karma. God, the ocean of power empowers us to do the right Karma. God, the ocean of love gives us unconditional acceptance which increases our self esteem. God's knowledge, love and power give us the strength to face the destiny; perform the right Karma now and reduce the suffering. This is his forgiveness and this helps to wash our past mistakes.

We need to be aware of the inner conversations going on in our mind while we are doing work which does not require our conscious attention. Driving, cooking, walking, getting ready all these routine works do not require our mind to be thinking about them. At such times our mind could be thinking about the past and the people or worries of the future. All these thoughts are negative karma and influence our destiny.

Respected Dongre Ji Maharaj used to say whenever your mind is free and not thinking consciously, start your JAAP. He used to say adopt any Mantra for your SATAT JAAP and start doing it whenever your mind is free, you will get rid of all sorts of negative thoughts. You will have no complaint against anything happening around you. You will not get irritated or angry and your mind will be cool and stable.

Some days later an accident happened in my life. I would like to share it with you.

"Once I was driving the car, going to a party in the evening at a time when sun was setting, my entire family my wife and three sons were in the car. Suddenly one electric pole stay wire on the road which was widened touched rear wheel of my car and car turned; all four wheels were up. The front windscreen had come out. After a few moments, I could come out from the shock and saw towards the other passengers in the car. I found everybody was alright. We all came out of the car through the way created by the removed windscreen. When we all came out lot of people assembled. I requested them to help me to get the car turned and get all four wheels on the road. I just switched on the car and it started so I told everybody to come inside and we moved towards the party. I remember that day as a result of positive thinking. Accident happened but did not hinder our happiness. The moment we take responsibility of whatever is happening we cannot undo, we can get rid of our negative thoughts".

Traditionally we have been taught how to work, how to speak, how to behave but we are never taught how to think. Instead of thinking what is wrong and what is right, we should experiment new things. We make our responsibility identified by the role; we have to think we are the soul and we are dealing with the soul, we will be performing our responsibility more humanly. Every role is a chance for us to explore new avenues. Let us surprise us with our own performance.

We concentrate on Karma but we become less attentive regarding our thoughts. Any thought which is creating negativity or even waste thoughts are not pure thoughts. We have to make our mind so strong that anything played on TV or cinema or elsewhere around us does not affect our mind and body. We should get detached. Brain cannot distinguish between real and reel.

Points to ponder

- We need pleasantness inside and pleasantness around us. We have to remember we are originally love, truth, pure, blissful and powerful. We have gathered dust because of our actions of past birth or weakness from childhood, family culture and traditions and experiences of life through many situations in life.

- We have to remove the dust and bring back ourself to our originality. This is making us vulnerable to situations and circumstances. We have no control on situations but we can control our responses to these situations.

- We blame other people and situation for whatever is happening in our life. We have to take personal responsibility of our reaction and responses irrespective of other people's behaviour or situations. Worry, stress, anxiety, etc are the outcome of our being spiritually weak.

- Life is not just about acquiring and acquiring only. In this process of acquiring more and more we develop a sense of fear of losing it. We develop attachment for these acquisitions and forget the basic purpose of life.

- Accepting is not giving up. Acceptance means that you recognize and understand your current situation. It gives you freedom to accept something rather than remaining in denial. You may accept or resist but can't change.

- Our body consciousness which creates separate identity of our body and status creates Ego. It happens when we allow our acquired success to overpower our inner strength. We have to achieve a stable mind.

- Blaming God, others or our past actions for our destiny weakens the soul power. We cannot change our destiny because it is the effect of our past actions but how we respond to the situation is the energy we are creating in the present.

- Our journey of self transformation is personal. Only we know what we were, what we are now and what we want to be. We cannot compare with others or get affected by other's opinions. We will have to take our own decisions.

- We have to concentrate on our thoughts. Every invention or creation is first created in thought. Creating waste thoughts, which is thinking about other people's, past or future, creating energy of worry, hurt or anxiety weakens the soul energy.

- Spirituality is not separate from our day to day life. Spirituality gives us tools like meditations, yoga and pure thinking which we can use in our family, professional and personal life. Actions done using original qualities of the soul are spirituality.

SCIENCE OF HAPPINESS

Quote from Sri Sri Ravi Sankar

"Don't postpone your happiness until some perfect future date. Be happy now tomorrow will take care of itself."

Life is full of events. Good or bad is our perception. We feel good or bad when we compare our times or our position and status with others. We have a general belief system that we should have faith that bad times are temporary, they will pass and good times will come again. We need to change this belief system as under this belief system we are passing the time with uncertainty and our expectations may or may not be met and we may make our times even worse. Spirituality teaches us that every event is fresh, new and beautiful giving us full enjoyment and happiness. We have to enjoy every moment without attaching any conditions to it and without wasting or expecting a better event in future.

Happiness is a state of being, created while working towards the goal, not a feeling to be experienced after achieving the goal. If we believe that happiness is after achieving, then we create stress, anger and fear while achieving and thus don't experience happiness. Before, I take the responsibility of those around me; I need to take responsibility of my own thinking and feelings. When

I am happy and take care of myself, then they all will be happy.

We have come alone and go alone so we will have to take our full responsibility. We should always remember that our first priority should be to take full responsibility of ourselves. Responsibility is my ability to respond. My responsibility is to control myself, my health, my happiness, my emotions and spiritual strength.

Whatever may happen in life we are here only to enjoy? Enjoy everything what so ever may be happening. Enjoy unpredictability, take it as surprise. When you come late in the night, enjoy your wife nagging. Problems may continue, but our enjoyment should remain. Unpredictability may bring hurt. If somebody calls you monkey, find out if there is any monkey around you, and don't feel hurt. If somebody calls you idiot, and if you are not then why should it hurt you and if you are, it is the statement of fact. In both the cases why should you get hurt and retaliate in the same fashion.

When you crack joke, people see your hardware and software but do not see your joke. One has to develop sense of WoW. Think if you don't have sense of WoW, you are missing a great experience of life. If your eyes are blinking, if your kidney is working, your heart is working, be happy and WoW. We have everything to enjoy. We have to be grateful to God only to enjoy. We are many a times burning from inside because of conflicts, jealousy, hatred, greed and all sorts of negativity, created by our past experiences.

We cannot extinguish this fire by taking external resources of putting water on it. But we can extinguish it only from internal laughs. So we should develop and enjoy laughs from inside. When we are unhappy we think others are the cause of our unhappiness. We have to balance between problems and joys. Let you overtake your difficulties. We have to renounce our belief system that we will be happy only if we do not have any problem. We have to think to be happy, joyful, in spite of problems. You must learn to laugh without waiting for the time when there will be no problems. Problems will remain, joy is your birthright. Cheerful mind discovers truth. Awaken your energy of joy moment by moment. It may be difficult initially but it is possible if you practice. You commit to yourself that you will be happy all the time.

We make certain goals in life and feel that we will be happy when we achieve our goal. Everyone has the same will power, it simply depends how we use it. We can get this awareness by SATSANG, DHYAN OR BHAKTI. We have to be aware how powerful we are. Environment and people around us also contribute to it. We are vulnerable; we have to secure ourselves that we are not affected by others. This can be done from Meditation, Satsang, Which makes us more and more aware and secures us from outside affect .My original SANSKARS are mine only. Family SANSKARS, Environment SANSKARS, PAST SANSKARS, are not in my control. My will power is in my control, but we have to be aware of our original SANSKARS. Instead, wanting peace think yourself full of peace, then, it will become powerful and natural

Our personality is a combination of 5 types of SANSKARS i.e. habits or traits.

1. Some SANSKARS we get from our parents and family, which we call hereditary SANSKARS. It is because we are in the influence of their vibrations.
2. Some SANSKARS we create because of our environment, our nationality, religion, culture and friends.
3. A very important SANSKAR we carry from our past birth and soul carries its personality traits created in one costume with it to the next costume.

4. Some SANSKARS are the ones we create through our own will power. We all have the same will power; it is only for us to use it, because each of us is a powerful being.

5. Some SANSKARS are the original SANSKARS of every soul which are purity, peace, love, bliss, Knowledge, power and truth.

Goal is going to take six months or so for its achievement. We are sure that we will achieve this goal in six months and will be happy. Now, we start our journey and find there is a delay. We feel it is because my people are not working as per our expected speed or they are not giving me full co-operation to achieve my goal in time. So we create stress that they are coming in between my achieving happiness. They are creating hurdles in my achieving goal, so my happiness. It will create stress and one will try to remove all those hurdles in the way, may be, he may have to move certain people by just blaming them creating wrong things or telling lies. So we will start losing our values for achieving our goal. We will create stress and fatigue this is all for achieving Goal and then happiness. So we have created all this negativity while in journey. So during these six months we would be creating all sorts of anxiety, anger, stress, negativity, loss of health etc and then if we achieve the goal; after six months we will feel happy. But think for how long you will feel happy.

Your success will motivate you to achieve further success and success. You will be setting further goals, even more difficult. So you will go on increasing your goals and stress. You will be trapped in rat race. So during the journey, we have created all negativity in us and around us taking all sorts of stress, compromises of values and making people around us stressful. So we are postponing our happiness on achievement and in between trying to achieve, achieve and achieve.

We are making all our family, our children and people working around us stressful. So, by the time we reach our destination, our emotional strength and power to deal with the situation will be weakened. It will increase our irritation. It will have effect on our body. You may feel less in the young age. Since, we have accepted this illness of the body also as part of our life we may not feel in the younger age. Supposing somebody is not getting job for six months and feels depressed, we advise don't worry, it all happens and it will come some day. Still if he feels depressed, then we have to advise that what will happen if you worry. Are your worries going to bring job to you? Same thing we should say to ourselves. People think that it is easy to say than done. But we should be aware that our worry will show on our face, our body language will change, our confidence will be shaken. We will feel demoralized, we will feel no enthusiasm. So we will have to take care of ourselves motivated and enthusiastic.

So most important is to set our responsibility. We are conscious that we have to take care of family, our job, our relations our friends, our country but we don't feel responsible for ourselves. We are taking responsibility of everybody but not taking responsibility of ourselves. Think, unless you are not happy and healthy how can you keep others happy. We have made it conditional that if everybody around me will be happy, I will be happy. Think if you are happy, you will be able to make everybody around you happy. Your happiness is your strength. If you are happy, you will get right thoughts, which will make you stable. If you will have negative thoughts, you will not be able to face the situations and you will not be stable. You will lose your strength and you will not be able to keep others happy.

Supposing we buy some beautiful jewellery of diamond and we create a thought of happiness and start responding to it that I am very happy but suddenly some person enters and says that it is fake; our thought of happiness is gone and so our response becomes of agony. So we make ourselves dependant. Our thoughts can make us happy or give us hurt. So we are making ourselves weak, dependent upon our thoughts, which are the outcome of circumstances and situations. We feel it is very normal that if something happens which we want or wish, we are happy and if it does not happen, we are sad. But we have to think that different people react differently in similar situations. Some people become so happy and some so disgusted in same situation and some people feel some happiness and some sadness in the same situation. So it is not the situation, which decides quantum of your happiness or sadness, but these are your thoughts only. So we have a choice.

We have to come out of this automated mode. Automated mode makes us machine. We are not machines, we are human being. The difference between machine and human is very simple. Machines have no choice but as a human being we have a choice. We can guide our reaction to a situation. We should not lose our power; the God has given us, full power to control our reactions to a situation.

We create around 25 to 30 thoughts per minute, i.e., 30000 to 40000 thoughts in a day. These can be classified into four types of thoughts. First type of thought is pure, powerful, positive, selfless thought. There will be no attachment or expectations attached. Second type of thought is negative thoughts of ego, anger, greed, hatred, resentment, fear rejection, criticism. Third - Necessary thoughts related to action, neutral thoughts. Fourth type are waste thoughts which are thoughts about past or future, both not in our control. Always be aware, your happiness is unlimited meaning thereby that our happiness is not dependent upon anybody, situation or circumstances. It does not depend on outside. It is internal, natural and from within only.

Achieving object or success is important, but not through any means. Means are also important. Success is achieved last in our journey of achieving our objects, if we are adopting unfair means, it will create fear, stress and deplete our inner strength. It will also not allow us to be happy internally, because we will always know within ourselves that we had adopted unfair means to achieve this success. So happiness will be incomplete.

Our belief system decides our way of living. We need to experiment what we are learning in order to change our belief systems. I don't want peace, but I am peace. Now I will be at peace and outside things will not affect my peace. Every person I meet; every act I do, I will do it with awareness - I am a peaceful being. Happiness is not dependant on people. No one can make me happy and I can't make others happy, till we want to do it for ourselves. No one is responsible for my hurt, pain, fear or anger. It is my own creation in response to their behaviour. I have another choice.

When we say we want peace, we have a feeling that we have an empty glass and we want to fill it. Think the other way, I am a peaceful person. I have my glass full, now I have to be conscience that I do not split it. I should not allow any body to split it. So we have not to ask for peace but we have to be careful that we do not lose our peace.

Always believe we have more capabilities than limitations. Our body is used to work mechanically and it has formed comfort zone. We are not machines; we are human being and are capable to do what we wish to do. We have to come out of the comfort zone and use our higher energy;

body is used to use lower energy because it is easy. For higher energy, we have to make some efforts. We can very easily with little practice come out of the comfort zone and make body habitual of using higher energy.

The amazing thing about life; you can choose how you want to react, how you want to respond, what music or tune is best to dance .It is all with us. We can choose to be happy or unhappy about the situation. Now a days uncertainty and unpredictability has become the way of life. We perform marriage with all pomp and show but still we are not sure how long it will continue. People are surprised to know if parents and their married children are living together. We have adopted automatic way of life, where we are dictated by the situation and we take reaction of the situation as obvious. We feel there is no other option. But we should remember that the obvious thing is only one; that we will react as we wish.

When people around us are in physical or emotional pain, we need to take care of ourselves. If we remain strong we will help to heal their mind. If we create pain, we will add pain to their pain. If we stop our negative emotions from coming into words and actions, we reduce their intensity and increase our willpower.

Excerpt from "The Dalai Lama's Little Book of Wisdom"

"The way our attitude works is such that it is often troubled by outside factors, so one side of the issue is to eliminate the existence of trouble around you. The environment, meaning the surrounding situation, is a very important factor for establishing a happy frame of mind. However, even more important is the other side of the issue, which is one's own mental attitude. The surrounding situation may not be so friendly, it may even be hostile, but if your inner mental attitude is right, then the situation will not disturb your inner peace. On the other hand,

if your attitude is not right, then even if you are surrounded by good friends and the best facilities, you cannot be happy. This is why mental attitude is more important than external conditions. Despite this, it seems to me that many people are more concerned about their external conditions, and neglect the inner attitude of mind. I suggest that we should pay more attention to our inner qualities. There are a number of qualities which are important for mental peace, but from the little experience I have, I believed that one of the most important factors is human compassion and affection: a sense of caring"

Points to ponder

- Life is full of events. Enjoy every event without wasting or expecting better events in future.

- It is my responsibility to control myself, my health, my happiness, my emotions and my spiritual strength. We cannot make our happiness dependent upon achieving something, or on other's behavior.

- We are burning from inside because of conflicts, jealousy, hatred, greed and all sorts of negativity created by our past experiences. We cannot extinguish this fire by taking help of external resources of putting water on it. We can extinguish it by creating internal laughs.

- We fix certain goals and targets in life and feel we will be happy after achieving our goals and targets. We create all sorts of stress in this process and postpone our happiness. We create all sorts of anxiety, anger, stress, negativity and loss of health etc.

- Success may bring temporary happiness but it will motivate you to achieve further and you will be setting further goals even more difficult.

- We make it condition for ourselves that if everyone around me will be happy I will be happy. Be aware your happiness is your strength; if you will be happy, you will get right thoughts which will make you stable and you will be able to make everybody around you happy.

- We have not to adopt an automated mode and become machines. We have a choice whereas machines have no choice. We can guide our reaction to a situation. We have full power to control our reactions to a situation.

- Always be aware that you are the creator of your thoughts. Always check whether this thinking is the right kind of thinking for you. And be firm that you can't change your thoughts under the influence of others just to please them.

- Achieving objects or success is important but not through any means. Success is achieved last and unfair means if adopted in the journey will always create fear, stress and deplete our inner strength. It will make happiness incomplete even after achieving success.

- When we do something for others, we should be very clear in mind that we choose to do it because they matter to us and so we are doing it for ourselves. We should not make our happiness dependent upon their response to what we are doing for them.

SCIENCE OF MEDITATION

Meditation is the key to obtaining organized mind, inner balance and spiritual awareness. Meditation is the process of re-centering our awareness in the principle of pure consciousness which is our essential being. Meditation means focusing on certain thoughts thinking of no other thought. One may do it by adopting certain mantra or thought or viewing his breathing or certain point in the body. This can be done once or throughout the day. Meditation is to witness the thoughts, actions and techniques like mantra chanting and breathing. It helps us to remain in the state of awareness and not flow away with the thoughts. This slows down the thought and leaves little space for negative thoughts. It stops depletion of energy and preserves energy. Ultimately, it is like saving meaning earning and spending thoughtfully.

Meditation will provide awareness so vast that it shall embrace all things, while simultaneously being the experience of freedom from all things. Eventually we are not held captive by our own mind; nor are we imprisoned by our own emotions. Meditation brings back our lost internal awareness of our true self due to constant focus on external objects validation etc and became habituated even addicted to ego centric or materialist consciousness.

We all have the potential to gain realizations in meditation: These potentials are like seeds in the field of our mind, and our meditation practice is like cultivating these seeds. However, our meditation practice will be successful only if we make good preparations beforehand.

If we want to cultivate external crops we begin by making careful preparations. First, we remove from the soil anything that might obstruct their growth, such as stones and weeds. Second, we enrich the soil with compost or fertilizer to give it the strength to sustain growth. Third, we provide warm, moist conditions to enable the seeds to germinate and the plants to grow.

In the same way, to cultivate our inner crops of realizations we must also begin by making careful preparations.

The Importance of Meditation

Stress Reduction

Meditation reduces stress. It has a direct effect on our entire nervous system by reducing stress related chemicals like cortical, and increasing the production of mood enhancing chemicals like serotonin in our body.

Health Improvement

Meditation improves our health by strengthening our immune system, reducing blood pressure and lowering cholesterol levels. It is one of the most powerful natural treatments for people suffering with insomnia.

Slows Aging

Studies have shown that the regular practice of meditation can slow the ageing process. The biological age of long term mediators is generally less than those of people who have never meditated. It is believed that the physiological cause of this is due to the fact that meditation helps to reduce the body's production of free radicals. Free radicals are organic molecules that are responsible for aging.

Emotional Stability and Positive Thinking

Meditation is a very powerful therapy for people who suffer from anxiety, depression, anger, ego and other negative emotions. People who meditate are less stressed, healthier, happier and they have a significant positive outlook on life.

Points of Practice

- The meditative practice of stilling the mind and developing insight into its true nature.
- Relax your body and relax your mind. First, make sure that all parts of your body are completely relaxed and at ease.
- Relax your attitude and your mood; make sure that your mental attitude, the tone of your approach, and your mood are also at ease.
- If you are relaxed and you have focused your awareness on yourself just sitting there, you have already entered into meditation.
- If you find yourself becoming drowsy, it is a sign that you are not relaxed or you may be sitting but not practicing, just resting.
- You are practicing being aware of the whole body just sitting there with all its different sensations as a totality.
- It will be natural if most of your bodily awareness is discomfort, but do not add any thoughts, feelings, or attitudes on top of that. There may be particular parts of the body experiencing pain or even pleasure, but do not localize or focus on those parts. Keep them in the context of the whole body sitting there. Just acknowledge that

there is pain or comfort at this moment, and maintain a simple knowing and recognition of that in your total-body sensation.

- Tension in certain areas of the body can cause the whole body to become unsettled or agitated. If this happens, please return to the relaxation method.
- The purpose of retreat is to deepen your relationship with your practice. To do so you must be able to settle within and not be distracted by (too many) worldly concerns.

Extending practice to develop meditation as way of LIFE

You can also integrate these principles into all your activities. Just as when you sit in meditation you just sit, when you sleep, be aware of the totality of your whole being going to sleep. When walking, you just walk. When you eat, you are right there just eating. Plunge your whole life into what you are doing at that very moment and live that way. So we train ourselves to engage our whole being in what we are doing. Whether sitting or eating, you are not engaged in discursive, wandering, or deluded thoughts. All of you—environment, body, and mind—is right there. Whatever you do, whatever the task at hand, your whole life is there at that moment.

Breathing

If you would like to achieve a peaceful state of mind, then practicing breathing techniques can act as a simple method to reaching these desired states. With each out-breath there is a sense of "letting go", of breathing without any goal. One should also not manipulate the breath. It should be silent, slow and relaxed.

Mantra

Mantra resonate certain specific positive sound vibrations that bring the mind to a state of calmness and peace. The purpose of sound in chanting is to bring silence in the mind through positive energy. When that happens, we find it easier to meditate.

The only way to get the amazing benefits of meditation is to practice as often as possible. Even if you only have a few minutes, try to meditate every day. The more you practice, the better you'll become at mastering your emotions and remaining calm. Schedule a mediation appointment with yourself every day and be sure to keep your appointment!

Various ways of Meditation

Understanding Vipassana

Vipassana is a meditation practice offered by Theravada Buddhism and follows the teachings of Satipatthana Sutta. It's a form of meditation that involves complete concentration on the body and the many sensations within to gain a deeper insight into self.

Vipassana is "looking into something with clarity and precision, seeing each component as distinct and separate, and piercing all the way through so as to perceive the most fundamental reality of that thing."

Understanding Zen

Zen is the Japanese variant of Chant, a school of Mahayana Buddhism which strongly emphasizes on dhyana. This gives insight into ones true nature, or the emptiness of inherent existence, which opens the way to a liberated way of living.

Zen meditation ideally is not only concentration, but also awareness: being aware of the continuing changes in our consciousness, of all our sensations and our automatic reactions.

Zen is a form of meditation that is usually performed in the lotus position. A seated meditative practice, it calms the mind and body and allows a person to concentrate on the 'inner flow of energies' that can shed insight on the nature of one's existence to gain a sense of 'Awakening'.

Difference between Vipassana and Zen?

Masters who have practiced both Vipassana and Zen will tell us that both of these are essentially the same, reason being that both these meditative practices focus on breathing and take you to greater heights of self-awareness.

However, some teachers point out that while Zen emphasizes on breathing deeply with the belly to reach a meditative state, Vipassana emphasizes on breathing through the nose to reach the state called 'jhana', which essentially means a series of cultivated states of mind, which lead to "state of perfect equanimity and awareness 'complete absorption'.

Additionally, Zen requires one to be seated in a specific position and is hence practiced for shorter sittings. On the other hand, Vipassana is more relaxed in regards to seating position and hence most Vipassana meditation sessions are longer.

Mahayana Buddhism teaches sunyata, emptiness, which is also emphasized by Zen. But another important doctrine is the Buddha-nature, the idea that all human beings have the possibility to awaken. All living creatures are supposed to have the Buddha-nature, but don't realize this as long as they are not awakened. The doctrine of an essential nature can easily lead to the idea that there is an unchanging essential nature or reality behind the changing world of appearances.

Quotes from Jeff Foster

"You will lose everything. Your money, your power, your fame, your success, perhaps even your memories. Your looks will go. Loved ones will die. Your body will fall apart. Everything that seems permanent is impermanent and will be smashed. Experience will gradually, or not so gradually, strip away everything that it can strip away. "Waking up means facing the reality with open eyes and no longer turning away."

Quotes from Robert Adams

"Always remember deep in your heart that all is well and everything is unfolding as it should. There are no mistakes anywhere, at any time. What appears to be wrong is simply your own false imagination. That's all. You are the Self that perfect immutable Self. Nothing else exists. Nothing else ever existed. Nothing else will ever exist. There is only one self and you are that. Rejoice!"

EGO AND INNER CONFLICTS

Quote from Sadhguru Jaggi Vasudev

"Don't think about money, think about living well. The most important aspect of living well is that you are doing what you really care about".

Power to withdraw and pack up makes us stable and still; connects us to our inner self and we will find creative solutions to our problems. For being still and stable, where creativity and solutions to the problems can be found, we have to internally withdraw for a few moments from the chaos outside and also the emotions inside.

First of all we have to practice to become same inside and outside. We should speak that only what we feel and do. When we practice and make ourselves the same from inside and outside, which means we speak only that what we think and do then our energies become harmonious. When our thoughts, words and doings are different we radiate conflicting energies which are less effective.

The next best technique to empower oneself is to adopt a nature of Let go. Let your past make you a better person than a bitter person. By letting go, we would be freeing ourselves from the pain. The more anger of the past, we carry in our heart, the less capable we make ourselves. While, living in the present very often we are thinking about the past, which could be many year old or just a few moments old. We create our present response and karma which then influence our future destiny. So holding on to our past influences our future.

Whenever, we feel that inner conversation of the past is repeating in our mind, we should be aware and create new thought of Let-go. Visualize the past impressions that incident had left on our sub conscious mind. We have to experience it repeatedly and teach our mind like we teach to the child, that we need to change our thinking and teach mind to have right thinking.

We should talk to other persons and that too not with the intention of criticizing but with an honest intention wishing the other person to be happy and by passing positive energy rather than negative energy and criticizing them. This is power to pack up and let-go. We have to be light in the journey of our life. These burdens of our past memories are burdening us and not allowing us to feel light and happy.

Whenever, we are letting go or forgiving anybody, we should not have the feeling that we are forgetting and forgiving and letting go the others. We should also think that others are also forgetting and forgiving us for our doings and are ultimately tolerating us. If we make list of things which we do not like of others, we will find that others are having even longer list of things which they don't like in us. So the need is just not tolerating others but is that of understanding others. We have just not to tolerate the difference, but should try to understand the difference.

Meditation is the best thing to move forward in developing power to withdraw and pack up. We have to prepare ourselves to face a crisis or interact with different people with different Sanskars and opinions. Meditation in the morning is an inner preparation for the whole day. In meditation we create a mental connection between the soul and supreme power which helps us to emerge the 8 powers of the Soul. These powers are:-

1. Power to withdraw from emotions.
2. Power to let go.
3. Power to accept.
4. Power to tolerate.
5. Power to discern.
6. Power to face.
7. Power to decide.
8. Power to cooperate

Upanishad tells us that as long as we search the reality outside us – we cannot find it. We have to turn within to know the supreme path.

So, we have to develop strength to withdraw from our emotions. We have so great influence of our emotions on us that we justify our energy act done as a result of our emotions. We develop belief systems, where we justify our every act based on emotions and we find ourselves helpless to act otherwise.

We develop belief system that work will be done only if I shout on people doing work. In this belief system, we are giving priority to work, not me, not persons doing the work. We have to think that we are doing work to be happy. Our belief system is that we will be happy on completion of the job or if the job is done properly and that will happen only if we take work from others even for that we may have to be angry.

We have to put brake to it, we have to think that I am the creator of my thoughts and it is affecting lots of people around me. We make life competition. We make our belief systems accordingly and start thinking and acting likewise.

We like people to deal with us with love because each one of us is a loveable being. So everyone around us would like the same. Every time we use anger as the tool, we experience the negative energy as we give it to others. They get hurt and their vibration of negativity is coming back to us. Our responsibility is to take care of ourselves, our people and then get the work done. Let's try a new belief system - Love is needed to get work done.

We get attached to the work. We see other's work. We start comparing with other's work. We start thinking work as me. So work becomes 'I'. We develop all sorts of jealousy and anger etc to see that our work becomes perfect. The whole energy doing this work is I. So, I have to be perfect not only in work but our way of doing work, people working along with us, and everything is our tool and we have to decide as I, how to use these tools. So, 'I' should be our priority. We should keep ourselves detached from the work. Work is not I. Work is for me to make me happy. But I am happiness and so I have to detach myself from the work.

To say 'NO' is the biggest tact but to accept it with positive reaction can't be just tact, it is 'SPIRITUALITY'. To say No at the right moment, in a right way and for a right reason is a great challenge. It is our old belief that we always want approval, acceptance and appreciation from others. We have created a comfort Zone, where we feel happy, when we get approval acceptance and appreciation from others.

Many a times we go beyond our capacity, wish to avoid saying 'NO'. We go out of our way to see that we may not have to say 'No'. We make our happiness dependent upon not saying 'No'. So we create stress we have to come out of this comfort zone. When we feel, that it is beyond our capacity or we don't wish to do certain things, we should learn to say No in an assertive way. We have to come out of our programming, where, we feel it necessary for our happiness to get approval, acceptance and appreciation from others. Sometimes we know from inside that we would not be able to do something but we are not able to say No, because others may not approve and appreciate it. They may see us as aggressive. It will create internal conflict. Thus, making ourselves unhappy and at the same time our conflict will reflect our unhappiness and we will not be able to make others also happy.

When we think that doing something is beyond our capacity or is not correct as per our perception, we should get convinced in our mind and then say No assertively. For example if somebody is offering you sweets and is insisting because as per his perception it is very good and he is offering you out of his love for you but you are having diabetes or you are following some dieting discipline, if you say No assertively explaining your perception, you will still get his approval and appreciation.

Spiritually speaking what we give others, we get. But the meaning of this is - What thoughts we give to others we get in return, because first we have to create those thoughts, so before giving to others we get those thoughts. People, many a times mistake it by thinking, whatever, we give to others we get from them. So when we respect or appreciate someone we expect respect and appreciation from them. But we should think that once we respect to others we feel respected because we have given respect. We have not to wait for their respect. We have to love others but not remain begging all the time for love. One has to make him independent for feeling good, without Approval, Acceptance and Appreciation.

Assertive and reactive 'NO' are different. Saying No, after understanding and appreciating the other's perspective, if said, this NO is assertive. But saying No out of Ego is reaction. We have to be honest to ourselves and should have courage to face the consequences of saying No, but say truth.

We can say assertively rather than critically. If we create critical thoughts about the other person but speak very sweet words, we are still sending them negative vibrations; slow down the inner conversation because it blocks our natural energy of happiness and love.

We have to get detached from the situation and keep no expectation from anywhere and anybody at any time. Be aware, always remain ready and open to amend. No expectation means - to be open to accept what has happened and don't get disturbed or become unstable. Don't just react to your expectations but respond, proactively, meaning be open to accept, if things don't go as you wished.

Points to ponder

- We have to practice to become same inside and outside. Our thoughts, words and doings should be same. We have the power to withdraw and pack up from any situation.

- We have a belief system that work will be done only if we shout on people. In the process we lose our health, create negativity in the whole atmosphere, set wrong example before our children. People work because of fear not with heart.

- Body is our instrument which we use to perform our duties. Eyes and mouth are the instruments through which 'I' the soul chooses what to do.

- To say NO is the biggest tact but to accept it with positive reaction is spirituality. We always seek approval acceptance and appreciation.
- The thing which we don't like to do we should learn to say No in an assertive way. Assertive and reactive No are different. Saying No after understanding and appreciating other's perspective if said, this No is assertive. No out of Ego is reaction.

BRIDGE THE GENERATION GAP

Quote from Millennial

"I have a lot of respect for the baby boomers thinking about the way technology and life was when they were children and how dramatically different it is now, it's insane to think how far they have come and how much they've had to adapt".

Quote from Sadhguru Rameshji

"The Eldest in the Family Should Not See Himself as Head of the Family but should see and feel as Heart of the Family".

Millions of children lose their parents in their childhood but still they grow because some people get the opportunity to find purpose of their life in growing them without any expectations; just to ignite their lives with inner happiness. Similarly millions of parents lose their children at the fag end of their life when they need them the most but they also get people who help them keep smiling and enjoying their remaining life.

This fact of life teaches that parents have got this opportunity to grow their children and ignite their inner happiness. Similarly it is the biggest opportunity for children to bring smile on the face of their parents, who have now got tired and need help. Both should not lose these opportunities. Parents by thinking that they have grown their children with expectations attached and children that they have become father of their parents and are taking the responsibility of bearing them till the time they are alive. This small change in the attitude can make the sea change in the lives of parents and children; the burden of responsibility would get converted in ultimate inner happiness and a feeling of Bliss.

Every parent aspires for the success of their children and wishes to make them better than them. Generation Gap is a unique example of how we can convert our happiness into misery. We for the whole life work for our children and future generation. Every generation innovate new things and evolves the society to be more prosperous. We try to learn from the past mistakes and try to give a new dimension to the society to make it a better place to live in. We wish to give more and more better education and environment to our children to progress and prosper.

The new generation gets the advantage of good work done by the old generation. They are benefitted by all the research and innovations which the old generations have done, but as they were all under process or just completed, the old generation could not enjoy the fruits of those researches and innovations in their generation. The older generation people have a sense of pride that we have given some such things to new generation, which they will get a better world to live in. They enrich themselves with lots of experiences during their journey of life. They wish to share that experience with the new generation. They also wish younger generation to use more and more new inventions and innovations. They also feel that they have given younger generation better education and lots of exposure.

In this whole process, the old generation creates certain expectations from the new generation. Certainly, with the benefits of old generation's hard work, researches, innovations and imparting better education and better exposure, a wide gap is created between the two generations in their thinking, in their knowledge and in their handling of different situations. The way of living also changes with new ways of living for better and more comfortable living. There comes a lot of difference in situations and circumstances. Working style also changes. With the complete change in the scenario, the old generation finds their experiences and way of doings, also many times, not adequate in the circumstances. The old generation experiences, what they have been doing for their senior generation or what were their expectations, may also change. What are the constraints of new generations and what is their thinking and what they feel of our expectations may also have sea change.

Generation Gap is a perennial Truth. It is there since times immemorial and it will continue to remain for all the times to come. Generation Gap is a natural process. It is, in fact, a sign of Growth, progress and continuous process of evolving new ideas. The Gap increases in geometrical ratio not in arithmetical ratio. So if two three generations before the Gap was less and now it is widening more extensively, so it is becoming more and more visible. Formerly, noticeable gap was created slowly in a period of say 20 to 30 years, and then the period was reduced to 15-20 years and then 10-15 years. Now this Gap is increasing at a very fast pace. There is a big Gap between three living generations.

Since, it is sign of growth; it is expected to be welcomed and should bring happiness to all. It should in no way, be a reason of conflict at any level amongst people of any status, age or thinking. But in practice, many a times, we see and experience that it becomes the cause of conflict and brings lots of unhappiness in our life. So, it is so unique that a thing which should give us maximum happiness and a feeling of pride becomes a big reason of our unhappiness. It forces us to think, how a thing which should give us utmost happiness is making us unhappy and is taking away our happiness to a great extent, making us most unhappy person.

When we introspect to find the reasons, we can find reason within ourselves. We have to accept that the difficulty is somewhere in thinking only. The introspection will tell us that it is mainly because of lack of understanding and tolerance. The main reason causing conflict and creating Gap is our expectations. The older generation thinks that their expectations are not met by the new generation; they are ignoring and not caring and have forgotten what they have done for them. Times immemorial, the society has been advising and preaching the youngsters to take care of their parents. The old generation expects younger generation to take care and behave according to their perceptions. There is nothing wrong in that but the old generation should think that expecting someone else to do certain things, which according to our perception is correct stems from an attitude of entitlement.

So, the main reason causing conflict and creating gap between two generations is their expectations and lack of forgetfulness. I think if we take certain measures to handle this gap, which ultimately is the biggest hurdle in achieving peace and happiness in life, we can fill this gap and make us proud of this gap instead of being sad or unhappy of this gap. We should always be aware that after achieving everything in life; still the biggest sorrow of our life can be conflict with our own. So it is very important for us to practice ways and means which may avoid creation of this gap.

Generation Gap may result in collusion between patriarchs and their brood in very prosperous families over anything from strategy to succession. It may bring its ugly face regarding ownership and property. It may happen when money takes over relationships. It is all about expectations how more can one expect to get. It also happens when value is not attached to the values of family traditions. This also happens as families move out of the larger home living together. They stop to communicate with each other and only information sharing exists. Differences may also arise about strategies of business and ownership.

We can look into the reasons for creation of generation gap and find the ways to deal with it.

1. Proper planning should be done when the patriarch is in control. They should communicate enough with junior members of the family, so that follow up systems may be in place.
2. The difference of opinion may arise because of different business environment between two generations. They should be discussed in constructive way.
3. The focus should not only be on who will succeed but also on the retirement plans of the incumbent for a successful transition to happen.
4. The patriarch should have clear idea as to what they should keep for themselves and what they should pass on, so that in future they have not to bemoan that they should not have transferred all their assets to their children while they are alive.
5. The younger generation should adopt themselves in communicating with their elders. Important business decisions may not just be communicated via a brief text message or sometimes not even that.

6. The succession planning should be through a process and not a one off event. The focus should not only be on who will succeed the incumbent but also on the capabilities of the person to see the business growing.

7. The younger generation will also have to make efforts to understand that old habits die very hard. So, they will have to work on them slowly and have to make some adjustments in their thinking also.

8. It is necessary that both generations should be aware that Generation Gap starts when old generation resists from learning from younger generation, who have better education and exposure, and younger generation forgets that whatever fruits of knowledge and new inventions they are enjoying today were sown by older generation.

9. The past cannot be erased and expectations cannot be surely, fully fulfilled. So the best way is to forget past and do not have any expectations and be in present only. Make mantra of life, remain happy, whatever, may happen, because we have limited fixed time, and that also is unknown. Positive thinking does not mean expecting good things always but accepting whatever is happening as it is.

Points to ponder

-   Children have always believed fully about the love of their parents. Parents should also not doubt their love and sincerity.

-   The older generation should adjust themselves and should try to make new generation happy as per their perception and not as per older generation thinking. Parents should not thrust their wishes and experiences on children.

- Younger generation should keep in mind that old habits die very hard. So they have to work slowly and have to make some adjustments in their thinking, while thinking of changing older generation as per changed situations and circumstances.

- Generation Gap is created only because the older generation resists from learning from younger generation and younger generation forgets that whatever fruits of their education, exposure and innovations they are enjoying today were sown by the older generation.

- Always remember creation of Gap between children and parents can take away the entire happiness from both and even after achieving all success in life we will be making our lives miserable.

- The Main reason of creation of generation gap is lack of understanding and tolerance The older generation should not feel their children as their investment attached with certain expectations.

MAN, THE MAKER OF HIS OWN DESTINY

Identify your hurdles/Limitations/Conditioning

Quote from Swami Vivekananda

"Talk to yourself once in a day otherwise you may miss meeting an excellent person in this world".

"This life for me is an endeavor to help people experience and express their ultimate nature. If you know how to keep yourself pleasant within, irrespective of what is happening around you, ultimate liberation cannot be denied to you".

Bayazid, a Sufi mystic, has written in his autobiography, "When I was young I thought and I said to God, and in all my prayers this was the base:

'Give me energy so that I can change the whole world.' Everybody looked wrong to me. I was a revolutionary and I wanted to change the face of the earth.

"When I became a little more mature I started praying: 'This seems to be too much. Life is going out of my hands—almost half of my life is gone and I have not changed a single person, and the whole world is too much.' So I said to God, 'My family will be enough. Let me change my family.'

> *"And when I became old," says Bayazid, "I realized that even the family is too much, and who am I to change them? Then I realized that if I can change myself that will be enough, more than enough. I prayed to God, 'Now I have come to the right point. At least allow me to do this: I would like to change myself.'*
>
> *"God replied, 'Now there is no time left. This you should have asked in the beginning. Then there was a possibility.'"*

Human life is beautiful and very interesting. We all have a level playing field in terms of our capacity. We have intellect and heart to think, observe and decide. We are having conscious and subconscious mind to play with all the time. Our consciousness drives us to be independent, pure, lovable and joyful. Our subconscious mind drives us to observe, compare and compete.

We from the childhood have a tendency to experiment everything. We read and hear lot of things but we want to experiment ourselves. No doubt, we are born alone, independent and will have to face this world alone. Our parents, friends, well wishers and others are there to tell us their experiences. They all are quite sure that their experiences are real. We all from the childhood are influenced by them. Under their influence we lose our independence and get attached to many belief systems. These belief systems start forming our subconscious mind. We gradually forget our originality and start acting on the instructions of our subconscious mind.

This tendency forces us, on every step to shape our lives according to the dictate of our subconscious mind. This sanskar makes such strong grove in our thinking that we stop seeking the other options which our consciousness tries to show us and we ultimately decide that we have no option and we succumb to the pressure of situations and circumstances around us.

Our mind is not our own. It is a complex amalgamation of all kinds of influences. The more we are identified with it, the further away we are from our self. The thoughts in the mind are created by the information we are taking in; our past experiences and our belief systems. We are influenced by external situations and then we process it through our perceptions formed on the basis of our information, experiences and belief systems. In this process we forget to see our self. We don't see dirt on our face and start cleaning the mirror. If we don't clean our face and clean the mirror only we will not be able to experience any change. If we don't clean our wind screen, while driving the car, the road and the traffic being the same, we may increase the chances of accident. Similarly we have to clean our behavior and habit every day to avoid accidents in life.

We develop all sorts of thoughts. We have to see every day what sort of thoughts we are generating. We have to analyze every day the quality of our thoughts. If we are developing negative thoughts, we will see that our internal happiness is depleting, emotional health is declining and then relationships will also start being affected. We very often examine our weight and see that if we are putting up extra weight then we are reducing our physical beauty, spoiling health and becoming less active. If we lose attention energy depletes and the peace goes. Like what you want to wear you choose; think and choose what kind of thoughts you want to create.

Human being means body and soul. Being is the energy, the soul. Today we focus more on doing rather than being. The original qualities of every soul are purity, peace, love, happiness, power, knowledge and bliss. We don't have to look for peace, ask for love, achieve or buy happiness; we are an embodiment of these qualities. I am a peaceful, loveable and Blissful soul. Give attention to the Sanskars which we want to be, Sanskars of peace, love and happiness; where attention goes energy flows, where energy flows things grow.

For creation of thoughts we will have to pay attention what raw material we are giving to our thoughts. First raw material is the information we give to our thoughts. When we give all sorts of negative news from Newspaper or News Channels– in the morning itself, we will give raw material to our thought creation process. If I have to become master of our mind, I should start its practice right form TV. Whenever we are seeing TV, watch it remaining cautious that it will not affect my thinking. This practice will enable us to control our emotions and thinking in the real scene or situation of life.

Law of attraction does not mean you get what you want. It actually means you get what you are. Our thoughts or words are what we are, these vibrate to the universe and we get them back.

What you are in a soul crying – Sanskars and Karmic accounts so what we are going to get will be according to our Sanskars and Karmic accounts. Thoughts create destiny, is always true for the soul, whether in this costume or an earlier one. Costume may change but the thoughts created then will still create our destiny. Destiny is created according to our qualities and skills of the present and also Karmic accounts of the past. Even if we are not getting the desired result, do not let any of the present qualities and Karmas decline. If we create jealousy, insecurity, anxiety, then we are creating a negative present. Accept the past carry forward and keep yourself strong and motivated in the present. If the present remains powerful and positive we will gradually settle the past and create beautiful Karmas which will influence our present and future.

There are lots of variations in people regarding their Karmas, actions and results. We have belief system that it is because of destiny. In this belief system we feel everything depends upon God. We have another belief system that it is because of the result of our Karmas or past actions. Both belief systems are very strong in nature. They will remain so. We have to constantly check our belief systems. We should be aware that belief systems create thoughts and they decide our attitude and destiny. Spirituality teaches us to experiment to try new belief system and see the results. We can't run both belief systems parallel.

We hear lot of things like them also but we don't experiment them. Unless we check them we cannot get advantage of it. We have to give some time to experimentation. When we believe that everything is happening as per wish of God, we always blame God and others for everything in life. If we believe that whatever we get is the result of our Karmas then we take care while acting. Thoughts are influenced by information, past experiences and belief systems. Every situation will be perceived through the belief system. Anger is necessary; happiness is in achievement; stress is natural; life is a competition; are some of our belief systems today. Even one wrong belief system reduces the power of the soul. It we held the belief systems – Anger is necessary; then we will use anger to get work done. Even if we decide to work peacefully, it will be temporary. We need to create a new belief system. Anger is damaging. Love is the way to get the work done. When we experiment with a belief system, check if – we are feeling lighter; health is improving; relationships are becoming simpler and Karmik accounts are settling. Then that belief system is right for us.

When a great Sufi mystic, Hassan, was dying, somebody asked, 'Hassan, who was your Master?'

'My Master was a small child. I entered into a town and a small child was bringing a candle, a lit candle, hiding it in his hands and going to the mosque to put the candle there. Just joking, I asked the boy, "Have you lit the candle yourself?" He said, "Yes, sir." And I asked, jokingly, "Can you tell me from where the light came? There was a moment when the candle was unlit, then there was a moment when the candle was lit, can you show me the source from which the light came? And you have lit it, so you must have seen the light coming — from where?" And the boy laughed and blew out the candle, and said, "Now you have seen the light going, where has it gone? You tell me!" And my ego was shattered, and my whole knowledge was shattered. And that moment I felt my own stupidity. Since then I dropped all knowledge ability.'

One must know the law and should have full faith in it and pledge to follow that in all the situations and circumstances. Similarly we should have firm belief system that we have come with some Sanskars and Karmic account. We will face whatever may come but will create good Karmic account and Sanskars. We will have to accept what is happening and move forward. If we take the responsibility and gather strength to face it; we will see that we will be able to handle the situation with greater strength. It does not matter how much we are in difficult situation, the thing which matters is that now we have understood and have started taking steps to rectify it.

Our every thought, word and action is the energy we create and radiate – this is our Karma, situations and people's behavior is the energy we receive – this is our destiny. We experience the energy of thoughts while creating them. Then they radiate and other persons also create the similar thoughts for us which we receive. So we experience while giving and also while receiving.

Karma begins at the level of thoughts. If we create negative thoughts but speak beautiful words and do good actions, we are still creating negative energy. Karma is not in the action, it is intention behind the action, i.e., the thoughts and knowledge of the law of Karma empowers us to create right Karma in the present. We take personal responsibility of situations coming to us; we don't blame anyone because we know it is return of our earlier Karmas.

Repenting is not regret of the past but it is the realization what I have to do now. So while repenting we have not to regret or feel guilt of it. We have to decide not to do it again. This realization will change us. Largely we have good relations with large number of people but have some problem in some relationship. So we have to take care of settling that past Karmic account. We have made mistakes in the past, may have caused pain to people around us, in this birth or past births. We don't need to think of what is already done, it's over, cannot be changed. Focus only on creating the right karma now. Creating guilt, self criticism or self hatred about the past will deplete our power and again create present Karma of negative energy. We need the power to create right Karma now, so focus only on the now.

When return of past Karma comes to us as challenging situations or conflict in relationships, we have now to respond to the situation with stability and positivity. Even if we are constantly receiving negative energy, we have to create and radiate positive energy only. Even if we have one strong negative Karmic account, it depletes the soul power and can affect our health and relationships. Change the quality of that

Karmic account so that we enjoy all our other beautiful Karmic relationships.

Life is a competition is a very old belief system but we should think that there are no competitions; we have to compete with ourselves. We have to think of improving ourselves only without competing with anybody else. Our target should be to achieve happiness rather than surpassing others. To competing for surpassing others is race and achieving our own targets is satisfaction. We have to choose between. It is only thought process which makes the difference. **Instead of thinking to be no 1 think of becoming 1ˢᵗ choice for your customer. For becoming no 1 you may have to adopt lots of means but to be 1ˢᵗ choice for your customer one has to focus on providing better service to the customer.**

Everything that we do whether at work or in family, let us set our goals and utilise our skills and qualities to achieve them. The focus should be on our own journey, not in reference to others around us. If we keep striving to go ahead of others and appear to be in race, then stress, anxiety, fear and jealousy will be our normal emotions. If we focus only on our goal, then there will be no in security; we will be confident and motivated. This stability will keep giving us the energy which will empower us to achieve our goal. When we create insecurity and jealously we will achieve less than our capacity. It is because we want to go ahead of others we compromise our values, principles and ethics. Compromising on values depletes the power of the soul.

Actually there can be no competition between two people, because two persons cannot be the same. Even if we assume everything between the two be the same, result cannot be the same for both. The difference has to be there. It is because of the affect of past karmas. We have to change our belief system and should talk of cooperation instead of competition. We should help each other, cooperate to move forward and make progress. If one will cooperate instead of compete will definitely go forward.

In studies business or any professional, social or creative activity, our resources, sanskars and skills are the present input parameters. Our past Karmic accounts are the invisible input parameters. Past karmic account is a powerful factor in deciding our success today.

Since our past karmic accounts can never be the same as of others we cannot compare or compete with others for our results. Questioning or being unhappy about other's success is a deep negative thought. When we start creating jealousy, insecurity, fear and low self confidence, then our present karmas also start declining. Focus completely on your present parameters and do the best to your capacity. Be satisfied with the results and continue to increase your capacity.

It is commonly said that people are born intelligent or talented. Everybody carries with him some genetic and past Karma's specialties. These differences between the two persons and old karmic accounts play vital role in their achievements.

When we create a thought it is followed by a feeling. This energy is experienced by us and also radiates to the person for whom it is created. Love means acceptance. When we get critical or angry we create negative energy of rejection. There is no appreciation, motivation or respect in those moments.

Our intention for family and friends are good, but in moments of anger our positive energy of love gets blocked and we radiate negative energy. Frequent blocking of our natural feeling affects our emotional and physical health and relationships.

The thoughts people create about us will always reach us. Any wrong karma invites negative energy from people towards us. If people are jealous of us they will create negative thoughts for us. If we create fear then we are creating negative energy and we will become vulnerable to consuming their negativity. Be compassionate for them they are jealous because they have achieved less than us. If we understand their pain and create pure thoughts for them, it will become a protective shield for us. If someone sends negative energy let us remember they are also a lot of people who send us blessings and pure energy. Focus your attention on the positive energy influence of the negative will reduce.

Whenever we try to make a paradigm shift from our automated mode that if anybody is talking or thinking against us and we think and talk to them positively, they will get impetus to behave more badly to us, we may not get instant results. We have to be patient and have faith in our shift of belief system, which is ultimately helping us to be more cool and peaceful.

Irrespective of the karma that the other person does always remember they are a pure, beautiful soul. This consciousness keeps our flow of love natural and radiates respect to them. When we have to give a correction for someone's mistake, it has to be given with vibrations of love. Negative energy from us makes them justify their mistake and they will not correct it.

We start our day with the thoughts we create in our mind it is not because of other's affect on us, it is only because of thoughts we create in us. The thoughts that we create in the early morning hours are the foundations for the day. So begin the day with reading or listening to pure powerful words and then churn on them and implement during the day. In case we start our day with meditation and nice Bhajan we keep something of that on our mind. Our thoughts create our destiny. Other's thoughts will not influence us if we don't accept their thoughts.

The thoughts we create are vibrations that radiate to the soul about whom they were created. These vibrations will trigger a similar quality of thoughts in them and those will then radiate to us very soon it is continuous exchange of energy. We need to be careful of the quality of thoughts.

The soul has divine sanskars and also impure sanskars. When we create pure thoughts, we bless our self and when we create impure thoughts we curse our self. God, deity or saints will never curse or punish us. When someone blesses us they are sending us powerful positive vibrations. When we take that energy and then create positive thoughts we have accepted and used their blessings.

When we take a decision it has to be according to our capacity to face the situation. We need to take the decision with full awareness of our sanskars which can make it easy or difficult for us to implement the decision. When we seek decisions or ask others for decisions it may go wrong. The one giving the decision is giving according to their Sanskars which may be completely different from the sanskars of the one implementing the decision. The right decision of the giver may be a failure for the one to whom it has been given.

Don't take decision for others. Be detached and see all the probable consequences of their decision. Show them all the options possible and leave the decision to them. Make others aware of their sanskars which they are not using. Empower them to use their positive sanskars to face the situation then they will take the right decision.

Every act which we do we are responsible and have to accept the consequences. We can never say that we had no choice. Everybody has the choice all the time. One has to choose and take responsibility. One can never say that they have no choice. Even at gun point one may choose to yield and the other may choose to die. One feels helpless only when he is weakened to accept it and is not ready to face the consequences. We take the shelter of helplessness for following any path which may be howsoever wrong. Everyone always has choice he is never helpless.

The more we ask others to take decisions for us our own decision making power will reduce. When the decision is ours we put in more than our capacity to implement the decision. We don't blame anyone instead take personal responsibility for the consequences of the decision and face them with power and stability.

People may have difference of opinion or habits. But it is not necessary that one is correct and the other is wrong. We are so attached to our own idea; own thinking and own belief systems that we think our self right and all others wrong. When others say wrong to our right we also start saying wrong to other's right. One cannot conceptualize anything beyond his experience or information.

Each soul's definition of right and wrong is based on their sanskars and their environmental conditioning. So in the same situation two souls will have a different definition of what is right and what is wrong. While giving advice to someone in conflict show them the perspective of other person which they themselves cannot see.

Even if you are in pain do not hold the other person responsible for your pain. When we blame it blocks our energy of love. When we don't blame it means we accept them completely. If we create thought for someone that they are wrong then very soon they will feel that we are wrong. Now both the people will reject each other and this is disrespect.

Points to ponder

- The thoughts in the mind are created by the information, our past experiences and our belief systems.

- For creation of thoughts we will have to be attentive regarding raw material i.e., information. We have to be the master of our mind.

- Repenting is not regret of the past but it is realization of what we have to do now.

- Don't compete with others. Compete with yourself. Don't think of becoming No 1 but try to become 1st choice of your customer.

- Take your own decisions; base them on your capacity to face the situation.

- Don't take decision for others. Show them all the options possible and leave the decision to them.

- Never think you have no choice, while taking decision. Everyone always have a choice. We take the shelter of helplessness for following any path, which may be howsoever wrong.

- Don't be judgmental. Each person's definition of right and wrong is based on their sanskars and their environmental conditioning.

FULFILLMENT THROUGH PEACE AND HARMONY

Quote from William Shakespeare

"Expectation always hurt. Life is short so love your life. Be happy and keep smiling Just live for yourself and before you speak listen; before you write think; before you spend earn; before you pray forgive; before you hurt, feel; before you hate love ;before you quit try; before you die live"

Quote from Swami Sukhabodhananda

"Happiness is part of our basic human nature but our mind creates misery. Misery is contrary to our nature".

We are Peaceful, Pure, Happy soul with love and truth as our strength. We are Happy Being. Worldly problems, situations and circumstances cannot make us unhappy. We are sometimes, swayed away by situations and circumstances and become unhappy and start blaming, situations, circumstances, luck and sometimes even to our children or parents, friends, and relatives, etc. We should all the time be aware that it is we only who can make ourselves unhappy. It is so simple, laugh away your problems, and you will be happy.

In our natural belief system we have lots of expectations from people around us. We feel it natural to expect from our family, relatives, friends or, whosoever, comes in contact with us. Expectations means wanting people to be the way we want them to be. Expectations are further created as to see that people should behave as we want them to behave. Whenever, these expectations are not met we start holding grudges and feel hurt. So, we create pain. So we must understand that pain and hurt is created by our expectations only, nobody else is responsible for this. We create grudges also because of our expectations. When we feel that family and friends are not meeting our expectations, we feel hurt and pained. We always see it from our perspective, we just forget to see from their perspective and we find it quite natural that they should meet our expectations in their behaviour and in their response to our expectations. This hurt created by us by visualizing things from our perspective radiates and generates negative energy to those whom we love the most, pray and wish for their happiness.

We also carry another belief system that we should always be conscious that we don't hurt anybody and we should act and behave in a way which gives happiness to all around us. These thoughts sometimes create pressure on us and in this process we forget our happiness. We should always remember that we cannot make others happy or radiate positive vibrations unless we are happy. We should never lose our originality. We should act as we like whatever, we do should not be just to please others. We should give happiness to others, but should first keep ourselves happy and then distribute our feelings of happiness to others, while, we should not keep expectation from others. We should not act always to fulfill other's expectations.

Let us do our best for each soul and radiate our purity and love to everyone. We have to live our life. If we live our life trying to meet the other's expectation even if it is not in our capacity, we may create pressure on us and in the process loose our happiness. Our unhappy state of mind will ultimately radiate pain to those whose expectation we are trying to meet. We need to think that expecting someone else to do something for us, is coming, from an attitude of entitlement, cannot become other's duty, gratitude and care. It has to come from within, with love and compassion.

Firstly, we have to be aware that we had come with empty hand and we will go empty hand. We have to detach ourselves from the worldly things. We will have to leave our desire to own and use ourselves, which we have built with our entire life's hard work. We have to be aware that we are no more capable of managing them. We may have lived in a house, built by us 50 or more years or any number of years, our children may have grown up in that house but ultimately someday we will have to leave that house. We should think what is going to happen to that house or property after I go. The best way is to secure finances by making it liquid by sale. You may even sell it to your children. The sale of such property will secure finances for you, which will save you from lots of hurdle and will reduce your expectations from your children and will develop a better atmosphere of trust and love in the family.

Secondly give those properties and assets to your children. Don't keep them waiting and don't live under the impression that they are loving or whatever doing for you is because they have expectations of those properties from you. This will spoil your all happiness which you will otherwise derive from the love and care your children are giving to you.

Thirdly - One should keep his finances as simple as possible keep one bank account, so that all your money and investment are available to you in a single statement. You should all the time know what you have and how you have to plan your expenses. You will have no worry on that front and if at all there is any worry, it will be in front of you. This will give you opportunity to address your problem and you will not live in a situation of uncertainty.

Fourthly - Your priority should be your health. Vital organs such as heart and brain are designed to work hard and for a long time. Even then if we feel any problem, immediate steps should be taken. We should neither avoid that nor postpone that. We should not expect others to take care of that. We have to take care and seek other's help without hesitation. We have to take regular care of our body limbs and stomach by ensuring daily walking, exercise and eating habits.

Fifthly - We should have open mind to adopt new changes, new inventions and new ways of living life. We should always nurture excellent relationship with our children, keep faith and full trust in your all relationships. Always believe that your children are taking full care of you. They love you and care for you. Be child, as they have believed you and trusted you, when they were growing up, you also believe them when you are growing old. Don't burden them with your care. It cannot be denied that we should live a life of gratitude. We should be grateful to God, our parents; elders and whosoever have done anything for us in life, but for God sake don't burden them for your care in return expectations. Always remember, you have cared for your children because you had opted for them. . It is simply your love and trust in them which will motivate them to take more and more care of you and love you.

We all need money, relationships and support system as we grow old. No doubt, we become physically weak but we can have our open mind and good thinking. We should not cling to our past. Don't ever give your children feeling of guilt that they are not able to take care of you or they are not meeting your expectations. Don't hold to your old assets. Keep your life simple. Keep your finances simple and handy. Take care of yourself and your health. Keep mind open to make arrangements where your care can be taken off without burdening your children.

A new concept of assisted living has been well developed. We should see if our circumstance so warrant we should not hesitate to avail these assisted living facilities. We should not avail them with the mindset that we have to avail them, as we don't have alternative, but enjoy them as the new beginning. Take it in the same spirit, when you had sent your children to hostel or abroad for their future and good living. You may miss your old home and friends but you will have the pleasure of enjoying new situations and new way of living and you will be fine with the change. Enjoy the change which will give you happiness. Love your children more as you miss them; send them feelings and vibrations of love without burdening them by creating negative feeling of pain. Since you have no responsibility enjoy this time as prime time of your life. You are a free bird. Enjoy this freedom with love for children and everybody in the universe.

This is not for older people only. This is for all who are growing old. They may be having lots of responsibilities and desire to make their career, wealth, property and other materialistic success. But always be focused that your perennial goal of life is happiness. While fulfilling all the responsibilities our prime responsibility is to remain happy every moment. You may amass lots of wealth and assets for your children, but you may in future never get such an opportunity to give love and care to your children, parents and elderly people, again in life. Your children will grow and may go beyond you to reach to them. You may lose your parents and this opportunity at hand may not come again in life.

Death is certain, life is time pass. We have to pass life happily. Don't get attached to anything, situations are passing, emotions are passing, elders are passing, age is passing and we are passing. We should catch which is not just passing. It is GYAN only which is always coming, retained, creating love and is liberating us.

I will like to share with you my personal experience of a real incident.

Success is not measured by material things alone. At any moment of your life the things which provide you inner happiness is the sunshine you brought into any body's life by your warmth, affection and compassion. Never miss an opportunity if you get to bring sunshine in any body's life.

"Once I got this opportunity. We in our family had a cook, who was with us since many years. He was around 40 and suddenly one morning he came from Ganges and shouted from the ground floor for having severe pain in his chest. I was around 30 years of age, heard the sound on second floor and came running to the ground floor; instantly saw him in great pain. I immediately called my family doctor, who examined him and said he is having severe heart attack. He examined and advised that the patient is not in a position to be taken to the hospital so we will have to create all facilities of hospital here itself. At the same time he also expressed that it is going to cost huge amount of money and may be by the time we arrange these facilities he may not survive.

Suddenly good sense prevailed in me and I told the doctor would you think like that if I am there in the patient's place. Doctor reacted immediately if you are so concerned please go ahead. Everything was arranged and by God's grace, he was saved and survived for more than 15 years after that. This incident even now after around 50 years gives me the feeling of bliss than any other incident in my life".

Points to ponder

- It is we only who can make ourselves unhappy. We create hurt lot of times because of our expectations. We expect people to be the way we want them to be.

- We should give happiness to others but should first keep ourselves happy and then distribute our feelings of happiness to others.

- We had come with empty hands and will go empty hands. We have to detach ourselves from the worldly things. Keep only that much which is quite enough to take care of yourself.

- Give your properties and assets to your children. Don't keep them waiting and live under impression that they are loving or whatever doing for you is because they have expectations of those properties from you.

- Keep your finances as simple as you can. Your priority should be your health. Keep open mind to adopt new changes. Be child, love and trust your children as they have loved and believed you when they were child.

- New concept of assisted living can give you the freedom of a free bird with no responsibility; new friends and new environment and can give you a feeling of prime time of your life. Love your children more as you will miss them.

- Persons growing old may amass lot of wealth and assets for their children, but they may never get such an opportunity to give love and care to their children and parents again in life. Children may grow and may go beyond you; may lose your parents and this opportunity at hand may not come again in your life.

APPRECIATE YOURSELF – A DIVINE SOUL

<u>Quote from Swami Vivekananda</u>

"Make your way of life as to how can you make other's feel nice; irrespective of his being rich or poor, elder or younger, we may have some interest of gain from him or not. If we make such criteria we will get rid of criticizing others because we will be focusing entirely on our behaviour. So we will compete with ourselves all the time and we will feel nice instantly. We will have its recording in our mind and it will become our way of life to feel nice and make others feel nice. We will never get time to criticize others or the situation. We have to be director and actor both ourselves."

We form certain habits and belief systems. We just follow them without caring how they are affecting us and others. Habit is working unconsciously. We are human being and are born with consciousness and intellect. We are special specie. We are expected to act, speak and behave consciously using our intellect and not be guided just by our habits and Sanskars.

The way we respond to a scene creates a permanent recording on the soul. Once a recording is created the chances of responding the same way in another scene increases and gradually that becomes our Sanskar.

The Soul is the actor performing every scene on the stage of this world drama. The personality of the actor will reflect in every role and every scene. Let us create the consciousness- I am a divine being and reflect divinity in my every scene today.

When we are role conscious we perform on the basis of our position, relation and age and expect the same from others. When we are conscious of the quality of the actor then irrespective of the role we will radiate our quality in every scene.

Ego is when we make something that we have acquired - our identity; it could be our qualification, our position, our skill, our relation or religion and caste. When we make any of these our identity we enact our scenes based on this identity and expect others to be with us on the same basis.

When the mind is hurt and is questioning other's behaviours, we cannot forcefully suppress the thoughts or silence the mind. The mind needs answers; give mind the answer that it is the other person's Sanskar and our past Karmik account, the mind will slowly accept and become silent.

This body is mine I am the power to use it. I am wearing this body, relations are mine, position is mine, wealth is mine, but everything which is mine will not remain mine tomorrow. So I have to use this properly.

The body is our instrument which we use. We see through the eyes, speak through the mouth, eyes and mouth are the instrument through which 'I' the soul chooses what to do.

We get attached to everything we acquire. Where there is attachment there will be fear of losing. Even though we know that eventually we will lose all that we have including our body, we spend our life holding onto it with stress, hoping we will never lose our body, family, position or property.

We have to think that we have acquired the body, relationship status, position, etc we have to take full care of it. But if we treat these acquired things as 'I' we will start to go overboard to acquire more and more and in this process we will forget ourselves that 'I'. So we will compromise everything to acquire more and more. I do all sorts of anger, stress and jealously so we will go out of perfection and beauty. 'I' wanted to be happy and peaceful, but we are searching this all in acquired things and are losing 'I'.

We need to acquire all our goals and take care of the acquired like a trustee but not made the acquired our identity. When we forget that 'I' am the soul, we start looking for perfection, happiness, power, love, which are the qualities of the soul in all that we have acquired.

When we believe that we are this body and we want happiness, we try to give happiness to the body. For happiness we go for holidays, buy gadgets, cars and clothes. We try to seek happiness in what we see, listen, smell, eat and touch.

When we believe that we are the role, we think happiness is in what we achieve; power is when people are in our control. To achieve this external perfection and power; we create stress, aggression, jealousy, insecurity, corruption and the soul moves away from happiness and power.

'I' the soul am bliss, love peace, power and purity. While taking care of our body, relations, roles and property we need to use these qualities in our every thought, word and action for the soul to experience peace, love and happiness.

When we connect to people as a role to role or position to position connection we radiate vibrations of ego. This creates thoughts of superiority or inferiority and radiates impure vibrations to the body and to the relationship and a permanent negative recording is created on the soul.

When we connect to the people on the level of soul consciousness we radiate pure vibrations which keep the mind peaceful body healthy, create divine relationships and earn blessings. Every recording on the soul in this state will be a clean recording and this recording is eternal.

Our consciousness or belief system is the source of our thoughts. We create 30000 to 40000 thoughts in a day. It is difficult to check and change the quality of every thought. If our consciousness is 'I' am soul then automatically only pure thoughts will be created.

When we are in the presence of a sole conscious person like a saint or a child, their vibrations bring us in our soul conscious stage and we feel pure and peaceful. If we are in a soul conscious stage we will enable others to emerge the divinity within them.

Not only in this birth, but for many births before this, we have lived in consciousness of body and acquired relations and positions, so body consciousness is natural to us. Sanskars of ego are strongly recorded on the soul. Meditation is the process of gradually creating a new recording of soul consciousness.

We need to remind ourselves - "I the soul am the master and these five sense organs are my instruments". In this consciousness we overpower our sense organs, but if we forget this then it feels like the sense organs overpower us because we do things which we do not want to do.

The thought created, if it sticks, it leaves its effect on our feelings and every cell of the body. It affects energy and weakens your mind and reaches to other organs of the body. The thought which we create affects other people with us also. That is why we feel peace in temple not because of its architecture but because of the people who visit their and generate positive thoughts. The thought creates instant difference in energy of the body. The negative thought instantly depletes energy. Positive thought makes the whole atmosphere positive and radiates the vibrations of energy.

Every place has an energy field based on the collective consciousness of the people there. Vibrations of a temple are different from the vibrations of a shopping Mall because of thoughts created by souls there. Everyone who visits there gets influenced by the energy field.

When we receive negative energy from another soul we have three options. We can absorb that energy i.e., create pain and hurt and suppress it within. We can reflect that energy i.e., radiate the same quality to others. We can transform it into positive energy and radiate to others.

The process is to absorb, reflect and transform. The choice is with us. If we absorb we create hurt. If we reflect we increase negativity. So, we have to transform the negativity into positive and radiate it to transform negative energy into positive energy.

The soul has three faculties mind, intellect and Sanskars. Mind creates different types of thoughts. Elevated thoughts are thoughts of soul consciousness are supreme thought. Positive thoughts are seeing the best in every person and situation. Neutral thoughts are necessary thoughts of daily routine. Waste thoughts are thinking about other people and thinking about the past or future. Negative thoughts are thoughts of stress, irritation, anxiety, fear or hurt. Toxic thoughts are hatred, resentment, harm or violence.

The thoughts of blame and negative emotions that we have been creating in response to situations have been recorded on the soul for many births. In meditation we create pure thoughts of soul consciousness and personal responsibility which come into action during the day.

The second faculty of the soul is intellect. Mind creates different types of thoughts in the same situations; intellect evaluates the thoughts and then takes a decision. The decision that the intellect takes comes into word and actions.

Our brain cells communicate with one another. One brain cell releases a chemical that the next brain cell absorbs. When brain cells communicate frequently the connection between them strengthens. Messages that travel the same pathway in the brain over and over begin to transit faster and faster. With enough repetition they become automatic. The more we think of a negative thought, the more entrenched the thought becomes. Negative and traumatic thoughts also tend to loop. They play themselves over and over until we do something consciously to them.

Information is the stimulus we receive through our sense organs. We take in this information and create thoughts. The intellect will evaluate these thoughts and take a decision. This final thought will be transmitted to the brain and then come into action. Similar habits of thinking will create similar actions and this will then go into an automatic loop which is called Sanskar.

We use addictions only to experience happiness temporarily, to feel energized, to distract the mind away from stress, hurt and negative emotions. When we use spiritual knowledge and meditation to heal our negative emotions, we will not need the addiction to feel better.

Sanskars once recorded in the soul cannot be erased. Soul has original Sanskars of peace but we constantly do not behave peacefully. We are not using that Sanskar. So it is like as it is not there similarly if we have Sanskar of anger, irritation etc, if we stop using that it will though remain but will be like non-existent. To prove and being obstinate is the sign of ego and leaving our thought lightly is the sign of soul consciousness.

What you listen normally forget, but if you repeat it immediately you remember 50%, if you tell it to somebody you remember 80% and if you practice you remember 100%.

We are required to change the concept of tolerance. Whenever anything negative is said or done to us we find it very difficult to tolerate it and feel why we should tolerate. We have to change our concept. We should try not just to tolerate it but we should be compassionate for the person who is behaving like that. He may have suffered sometime in his past and may have developed this Sanskar.

Whenever any good thing happens we are happy but when something bad happens we feel "Mere Saath hi aisa kyun hota hai". It is most surprising when people suffer they ask why me? When they prosper they never ask why me? God doesn't write our destiny we write our destiny. If God would have written destiny for everybody he would have written good destiny for everybody, as he is father of all and takes care of all his children. We form our destiny by our Karma. Karma of even previous Janmas affects our destiny. We start believing other things as cause of our destiny. Vastu, Astrology, Good time, Bad time, all are science but they are all of lower energy. We have to believe in super energy which is our soul. We have to strengthen our energy of soul.

Sometimes, we keep silence, even if we are not liking what other is saying or doing. Keeping silence may be by not speaking by mouth, but if the thing is there in our mind, then we will continue having negative thoughts. So, we need to not only be silent by mouth but in mind also. We may have not liked someone's behaviour but we should continue sending good vibrations to him.

The outside situations are there but we have to deal with them ourselves. Situations may be roller coast, full of difficulties but to be happy or sad is with us.Life is not a series of situation and scenes which comes to us. Life is our inner state of Being, based on which we respond to every scene. The quality of our response creates our experiences and that becomes the quality of our life.

For the same series of situations, same challenges and obstacle, different people will respond in a different manner. For the person who creates stress, anger and fear, Life will be burden. For the person who crosses it with ease, acceptance and love, life will be a beautiful journey.

The more we blame people and situations for how we feel, the more we will cross every scene unaware of our responsibility. When we take personal responsibility for our state of being, attention will be only on what we create, irrespective of situation. If we are calm and stable on our journey of life, our vibrations give cooperation and support to others around us to make their life a beautiful experience. Our vibrations help them to emerge their divinity in response to situations.

Points to ponder

- We should be director and actor both ourselves. We should take personal responsibility of our state of being. Attention should always be on what we are creating, irrespective of situation. Our vibrations give cooperation and support to others to make their life a beautiful experience.

- Ego is when we make something acquired as our identity. We acquire position, relations, property and skills and make them our identity and get attached to it. We create Ego. Ego is attachment to a wrong image of our self.

- My body is for me and I am not the body. When we try to make our body to look good we develop inferiority complex, jealousy and other evils in comparing ourselves with others.

- Whatever we have acquired, we have to take care of that as trustee. But we should be aware 'I', the soul am bliss, love, peace, power and purity. While, taking care of our body, property, relations and roles we need to use these qualities in our thought, words and actions for the soul to experience peace, love and happiness.

- We have inner consciousness different than our mind. The choice is with us to give permission to mind to accept what inner consciousness is saying or go ahead with its thinking.

- When we receive negative energy from another soul we have options; we can absorb; create pain and hurt and suppress it within we can reflect it; we can transform it into positive energy and radiate to others. The process is to absorb, reflect and transform. The choice is with us.

- What you listen normally forget, but if you repeat it immediately you remember 50%, if you tell it to somebody you remember 80 % and if you practice you remember 100%.

- Blaming people, situations or past or the world or our destiny or sometimes God for how we feel is the prime reason for depletion of our soul power.

SELF ANALYSIS

From "Silence in action" by Vimala Thakar

"Do you know how much energy is wasted in the chattering of the mind? Every thought consumes energy. Every emotion consumes energy. Even, when you are physically alone and by yourself you could be spending lots of energy through the chattering of your mind. The chattering which consumes energy will have to come to an end. Energy should not be wasted in reactions. Reacting and brooding also imply consumption of vital energy. Unwarranted indulgence in thought and emotion is sheer waste of energy. So please find out how much energy you are wasting throughout the day. If you allow that energy to gather itself unto itself, you will have immensurable more energy"

Every human being has born with inner strength of soul having seven powers in it. Peace, Love, Purity, Power, Knowledge, Truth and Wisdom. These are every body's original Sanskars. Every human being has also born with his past life Sanskars. In this life he gets family Sanskars, Sanskars through environment in which he is living and he creates certain Sanskars through his will power and his own experiences. So every human being is having seven inner strengths, they are his original Sanskars, but during the journey of his life, he is influenced by other Sanskars also.

These original Sanskars and other Sanskars are the wealth of a **BEING**. During this journey of life he also accumulates the other monetary wealth. Every human being possesses two types of wealth.

- Monetary Wealth
- Spiritual Wealth

There are lots of ways and means we have devised to assess and analyze our worldly monetary wealth. We are very vigilant about our monetary wealth. We are making all efforts and utilizing our all energies to increase this wealth. We are always gazing whether it is going up or down. We many a times think that our entire happiness, friendships, relationships and even prestige in the society depends upon this wealth.

Normally, we are not so sincere and vigilant about our spiritual wealth. We are not consciously working to increase our spiritual wealth. We are not making sufficient efforts to increase the strength of our soul. We have a belief system that we are not capable of analyzing our spiritual wealth. We also feel that it is not in our hands to strengthen our soul and increase our spiritual wealth. We also do not believe that we and we only can increase or deplete this spiritual wealth. We don't accept that we can increase or deplete it through our KARMAS. We also can't think that we are affecting this wealth every day through our Karmas. We feel that it is only God given and it can be increased only with his blessings. We don't think that we can deplete or increase it through our Karmas and we have a need to analyze it all the time. We just don't know this art, because we don't accept that our behaviour many a times is depleting this wealth and we should make conscious efforts to check it by changing our Sanskars and remembering our original Sanskars. SAINTS and SADHGURUS have told us very good way of analyzing and keeping constant watch on our spiritual wealth. We have to be conscious of the fact that we want to know whether our inner strength is depleting or increasing.

As a matter of fact, if we sit calm for just 10-15 minutes and meditate; how many times we are getting trapped by the situations, when we are getting anger, getting tempted or feeling jealous of others. How many times we are getting hurt or cheated. How we are losing trust in people and doing some actions, inflicting loss or hurt to others. We would discover that almost every day we are doing something or the other. The best way to analyze this strength is to be conscious that how much we are dependent on others to provide us happiness and peace. How much we are controlling our mind and are conscious to derive happiness and peace to remain pure, quiet and calm from within. How much our behaviour is influenced by other's behaviour? How much the circumstance, situations and other's attitude and behaviour towards us are controlling our mood or happiness. How many times we are getting angry or getting tempted or feeling hurt or jealous by the outward factors. How much and how soon, we are feeling hurt or cheated. How many times or quickly we are losing trust in people. How we are creating distances in our close friendships and relationships. How our behaviour or actions are causing hurts or inflicting loss to the others, which is depleting our inner strength or spiritual wealth. Actually this introspection scares us to analyze this spiritual wealth.

So first of all we should not bring guilt in ourselves if we are getting trapped to these things. We should make a list of these causes of depletion of our inner strength and we should find out the ways to counter this by adopting means and ways to increase the inner strength.

Once, we identify the reasons of depletion we can work on them. We will find that it is not very difficult, not something beyond us to reduce this depletion. The simple thing is awareness and determination. Take for example anger. We are very often getting angry on some people but at the same time we are not getting angry on some people. It may so happen that in both the situations, behaviour of others may be almost same. Similarly in some situations, we get tempted and in some we don't get tempted. Sometimes we are hurt because of very small things and sometimes we are not hurt, even if somebody throws lots of abuses on us. Sometimes, we quietly tolerate some person's behaviors and sometimes we react immediately against some person's actions or behaviour.

We need to understand this how we are having split personality. In the same situations, under almost same circumstances how our behaviour is different. How it is happening. We will immediately be getting reply; it has got something to do with our inner feeling or our inner actions, which is causing this. Situation or circumstances are not cause of it. It will be very easy to understand then it is we and we only who are giving permission to ourselves, in some cases getting affected and in some cases not getting affected. In some cases we are getting affected instantly.

We develop belief system that we cannot tolerate any nonsense and to get angry is natural. If somebody is not behaving property we are bound to be angry. There are some people if you don't scold or be angry will never perform. We also believe that if there is something good it is natural to get tempted. If we are feeling acute shortage of something and somebody is just spending it in plenty and not minding even wasting it, it is obvious we will feel jealous. If somebody has behaved in a manner we feel is very wrong as per our perspective, we are bound to get hurt. Similarly, we feel cheated or losing trust in people as common things happening in a very natural way.

We have simply to get out of this belief and think, these things may come in a natural way but I have the choice and power to see that they don't affect me. I always have a choice to be angry or not, to get tempted or not, to feel jealous or not, to feel hurt or not and to lose trust or not. Once we understand our power and know per sure of the choice then we will start making choice and very soon we will understand ultimately, what choice I should make, which will be best for me.

I am sure, if we start thinking in this way, very soon, we will discover that we are gradually reducing the emotions, which are denting or depleting our inner strength or spiritual wealth. Once the depletion is stopped or reduced, the spiritual wealth which is there in abundance, because that is our original treasure, we are like that, we will come in our originality and we will be awakened.

The first thing required is we should be fully convinced that for our happiness, it is of utmost importance that we become original, pure, truthful, peaceful, and powerful and love everybody. Once, we are convinced and start trying to be original. We will start analyzing and then we have to believe that we are the original. We have simply to remove the dirt. We will stop thinking that it is easy to say than done. We will start practicing and doing. Soon, we will start realizing everyday that we are able to remove dirt. We are coming in our originality and are able to remain happy.

Everybody wants to be honest. But sometimes circumstances create different definition of honesty in our mind. We mould the definition of honesty as it suits us. The meaning of honesty is very simple. Courage to face the

TRUTH is honesty. Honesty is inner cleaning. Sometimes we speak for others. We speak what we do not mean. We may speak lots of things to be polite, humble and be good in other's books, but from inside we don't mean that.

Honesty is speaking out the mind which we feel from inside. So we should always remember that we have to be honest to ourselves. We cannot deceive anybody whenever, we have to say anything we should first start feeling that. Keeping conflict inside sends two messages. The relationships based on such behaviors cannot develop an honest relationship. We should just not try to make other people happy but should do whatever we can do happily. This will send right vibrations. You may be extending courtesy but if it is not from inside, it will appear to others as false courtesy.

We must always ask ourselves, are we honest in our behaviour. Are we saying that thing only which we feel like, and comfortable to us, what I think and what I mean? Encourage people to say what they feel. People should know you as one who speaks only that what he means. If first you develop it in yourself you will be able to understand others.

You do what you think, I do what I think. Do everything which you feel like doing. If you have to do something, first start thinking to do that then do. So you have to change your thoughts, convert them into feeling and then do. I have to go, though, I do not feel like going but still go, is not integrity. If you have to go, start feeling to go and then go, is integrity. So you take yourself with you, while, speaking or doing anything. Integrity is to keep mind and body together creating harmony within you.

Unwanted behaviour –

For me some behaviour may be unwanted behaviour, at the same time others may feel our behaviour unwanted behaviour. We don't compromise in action but compromise in our mind. So conflict remains. It can be eradicated only if we want to resolve. We have to stop thinking not only talking or doing otherwise the negative energy will continue to pass to the other people.

Tension is replaced by stress. It has become status symbol how much you are stressed. If you are not stressed, it means you're not doing anything.

Fear of the unknown is the sign of weakness of Atma. We have to increase the immunity power of our Atma. Give advice but don't think that others should accept our advice, if the other person does not accept, we feel sad and send negativity.

Give advice as Malik and become child after giving advice. No expectation after giving advice. Give advice with love and respect with no expectation that it will be accepted. It is easy to expect others to change but we know we can't change instantly.

Don't teach your children to be smart but teach them to be compassionate. Don't teach children to face the world but train them how to make the world beautiful. If you want to create any Sanskar first get them in you and then it becomes culture of the family.

God has made everybody different. Every person or soul is different. We have to accept everybody as they are. We sometimes feel acceptance as weakness. When we accept we don't create thoughts against the other person. Treat it as natural. If you accept without creating negative thoughts you will not feel weakness. If your thinking is having questions for everything, you will not be happy. Our mind is always questioning and not accepting. We should first silent our mind and don't think of questioning anything then only we can achieve happiness. Our role is to empower our children or anybody whosoever come in touch with us.

Accepting another soul means understanding that they have their Sanskars and not creating any negative thoughts about their Sanskars. Acceptance lets the mind remain calm and stable.

Telepathy is experienced by people many a times. Now scientifically it has also been proved that things reach mind to mind may be sitting thousands of miles away. We feel it happens sometimes only. As a matter of fact it happens all the time but we realize it only sometimes, as we are having lots of things on our mind.

Spirituality and science both believe that all thoughts created by us for others travel but they are felt only when we are remembering that person. So we have to be careful of our every thought. We may be thinking that our negative thoughts will not reach to the other persons.

Balance sheet of life: Let us visualize our journey of life whether it is going as we wish or plan. Sometimes, we work very hard and don't get success. Sometimes we work less and even then get success. Sometimes people betray us whom we trusted most and some people give us unexpected support. It is very rare that we get the same which we script. Lot of time happening is quite different than what script we write.

We must learn how to perform better and remain positive and optimistic:

1. We have to rewire our brain to be positive. We have to train our brain to be optimistic in dire situations, even as things go out of control. It is natural and normal to have negative thoughts, but we must not let them influence our decisions. The best way to remain positive and optimistic is to count your blessings every day. We forget to show our gratitude towards our friends and family members. We take their blessings for granted. We many

times share only miniscule negative points of our lives. We should always ask ourselves what is in our lives for which we are grateful; it will change our thinking.

2. Do what you love the most at least for 15 minutes every day. Doing something you love will help you stay positive even if it does not pay you. As we grow up, we forget that the whole purpose of living is to stay happy at this present moment.

3. Think of bringing smile to somebody's face. Don't focus on the bad in the world around you and be focused on the work you are doing. So look around how you can bring smile on somebody's face.

4. Express your love for someone every day. Expressing love by saying, gifting, helping or even shouting will increase your happiness, boost immunity, and reduce anxiety, depression and increase feelings of connectedness.

5. 'Live well' – For living well you need not to worry if money can't buy happiness. For living well the biggest influencing factors are good sleeps, sex life, job security your strong relationship with your friends and family and good health of you and your loved ones.

6. Controlling of emotions specially anger. No doubts it's difficult to get rid of anger we come across almost on a daily basis. Spirituality strengthens us to control anger. We can also practice penning down our all emotions; start writing as soon as you face an anger provoking situation. Expressing one's feelings on a sheet of paper can cool the brain and help perform the task more efficiently.

Points to ponder

- We assess our monetary wealth but we are not yet so sincere and vigilant to analyse our spiritual wealth. We feel we are not capable to analyse our spiritual wealth. We have to be conscious that we want to know whether our inner strength is depleting or increasing.

- Every day we should sit calm for just 10-15 minutes and meditate during the day to know how many times we were trapped by situations.

- We should not have guilt in ourselves if we are trapped to these things. We should make a list of causes of depletion of our strength and think about the ways to counter them to increase the inner strength

- We have the strength but simply we have to take care of our split personality. We create different responses and reactions with different people in similar situations.

- We have to be honest with ourselves. We should speak what we feel from inside. We should just not try to make other people happy but should do whatever we can do happily.

- We sometimes feel accepting people is our weakness. But remember if we accept somebody without creating negative thoughts about him we will not feel weakness.

- We should advice people with love and right intention without caring whether our advice is accepted or not. We should always believe that people will change as per their thinking.

- Be positive. The best way to remain positive and optimistic is to count your blessings every day.

- Do what you love the most at least for 15 minutes every day.

- Live Well. Think of bringing smile to somebody's face. Express your love for someone every day. Have good sleep and good health. Control your emotions.

If you plant honesty, you will reap trust.

If you plant goodness, you will reap friends.

If you plant humility, you will reap greatness.

If you plant perseverance, you will reap victory.

If you plant consideration, you will reap harmony.

If you plant hard work, you will reap success.

If you plant forgiveness, you will reap reconciliation.

If you plant openness, you will reap intimacy.

If you plant patience, you will reap improvements.

If you plant faith, you will reap miracles.

But:

If you plant dishonesty, you will reap distrust

If you plant selfishness, you will reap loneliness.

If you plant pride, you will reap destruction.

If you plant envy, you will reap trouble.

If you plant laziness, you will reap stagnation.

If you plant bitterness, you will reap isolation.

If you plant greed, you will reap loss.

If you plant gossip, you will reap enemies.

If you plant worries, you will reap wrinkles.

If you plant sin, you will reap guilt.

BE HEALTHY

"Health is a state of complete physical, mental and social well-being and not merely the absence of disease or infirmity" - World health Org.

From "Journey into Healing"
by Deepak Chopra

"An old Indian saying goes "If you want to see what your thoughts were like yesterday, look at your body today. If you want to see what your body will be like tomorrow, look at your thoughts today

It is our prime responsibility to be healthy. We must be healthy physically, mentally, emotionally and spiritually to enjoy this beautiful human life. The diseases which can make us sick and come in as obstacle in the joyful journey of our life can be classified in four broad categories.

1. Genetic related.
2. Life Style related.
3. Emotional related.
4. Infection Related

The genetic related diseases can be controlled and cured by taking certain precautions and preventive measures. Life style related diseases can also be controlled by amending our life style with the help of professional experts. But emotional related diseases like depression; suicide tendency, bipolar disorder, Schizophrenia, dementia, addiction, sleep disorder

Etc. can be cured by adopting spirituality. As a matter of fact for taking preventive measures to control genetic diseases, or determination to amend lifestyle and to regulate emotions we require to develop spiritual strength. Diseases acquired through infection are external and can be cured by external help through medical science. We have to be confident to feel all the time that I am healthy. I do not suffer from any disease.

Some people are overworked and because of that they are ill and some people are less worked because of that they are ill. You have to use the body to keep good health. 80 % of illness is because we are not using our body properly. 10% is because of Karmik and remaining may be because of other reasons. Health is not to be invented. Health is not an idea created by us or anybody. It is a natural function of the body. If we will allow the body to function in a natural way it will be healthy. It is not a medical idea. It has become important because we are more and more becoming unnatural and so we are becoming unhealthy. We have increased the lifespan by taking extra care of the body clinically. But living long does not mean we are living healthy life. One has to remain healthy and enjoy long life by using his body properly and taking care of his eating habits.

Body exercise, Food habits, mental body – (Physical, Bliss body) are required to lead a happy healthy life.

Physical, Mental and Energy body to be aligned to a proper balance then there will be no physical or psychological illness and you will become blissful and that will be your natural process.

Food Habit - How quickly it gets digested. It has to be digested within three hours. Keep a gap of 5-6 hours between the meals.

Body Exercise - Bending, forward, backward and stretching, sideways is the normal function of the body.

Primarily, all diseases, especially emotion related are self created. The most powerful emotion related diseases are Depression and EGO. They, many a times, become so disastrous that they affect the whole life and we do not find their treatment anywhere in any medical science, whether it is Naturopathy, Ayurvedic, Homeopathy or Allopathy. They can be treated only by KARUNA of some SADHGURU. Because depression and EGO are self created and can be treated by ourselves only. It is Guru only who can enlighten us and make us aware of ourselves and can spiritually strengthen us to get cured from these diseases.

We are capable of causing depression to ourselves. It is natural that we have the power to generate the intense emotions and thoughts but in the wrong direction. So, when we are creating strong thoughts and emotions which are not for our good but bad for us we cause depression to ourselves. Most of the illnesses are self created only a few diseases are because of genetic or infection. For diseases created by infection we can always take the help of professional doctors but for the rest of the disease which are self created we should take the help of some spiritual guru. Almost everybody if gets victim of different types of emotions, they can go mad. The line between madness and sanity is very thin. When you're angry you are pushing your line, from sanity to madness. After sometime when you control your anger you come back to sanity from madness. But if you continue pushing that line all the time, someday you will not be able to come back and become ill and need a Doctor. A stage will come when you will not be fully ill and so your friends, family and others will have to bear you before you become fully sick and then they can get rid of you by dumping you in asylum.

In the childhood you become physically ill to get attention of the people, if you are married you get mentally ill to get attention of your wife or husband. So 70% of our illness is self created. So we have to create incentive for being healthy for ourselves and our family. We must understand that we have to work to remain healthy. We have to create necessary conditions and incentive for good health. We have to give best attention to us and our family member to make them and ourselves joyful. We must understand mentally, physically and psychologically that we get best attention only when we are joyful. We will be able to train everybody inside to learn this and they will all behave properly and we will be healthy all the time. Fear is because we are not living in life, but we are living in mind. So we are having fear of a thing which does not exist. We are not routed to reality. We are living either in past or imagination. They both don't exist and so we develop fear because we are not living in reality but are living in mind, thinking of worst and imaging lots of things.

When we create energy of anger and hatred, we will not feel love and respect if we are receiving it from others, because we are enveloped with our own vibrations. Repeated patterns of a particular thought like - whether a task has been done properly, have I made a mistake; have I hurt someone; will I fall ill. If any of these thoughts continue coming repeatedly many times a day then it is called obsession.

When an obsessive thought comes into action like - washing hands, having a bath, checking the door, checking the Gas or checking switches and are performed repeatedly then it is called a compulsion. This is OCD, obsessive compulsive disorder.

Spiritual counseling and psychiatric treatment can treat OCD. Spiritual insights and family can help the person to create a thought which counters their obsessive thought, and gradually change the obsessive thought pattern.

Depression:

Mostly depression is self created. One having very intense emotions is capable of creating depression for him. People get depressed because their dreams are not fulfilled. Their inner experience is determined by the external factors. World cannot be and should not be 100% what you want it to be. What you need is 100% pleasantness inside and for this you need nobody's cooperation. One is not at peace when his intelligence is working against him.

Ways to healing depression:-

1. Desire to be happy inside by reducing your external desires.
2. Mediation – Make yourself calm.
3. Be with happy people.

Medicine for depression is habit forming; they slow down our normal functioning; they make us sleepy; treatment goes on for years without much result - These are all myths. Depression is completely treatable with guided meditation and therapy. Practical application of spiritual knowledge in our way of thinking along with medical supervision helps us to change our thought patterns and come out of the episode of depression. Spiritual insights empower us and help to prevent recurrence of depression.

A person suffering from depression should not meditate for long hours or sit in silence since, the mind tends to go into its cycle of negative thinking. Thoughts of feeling inferior because of childhood comparison or failure to perform, feeling rejection because of failure or abuse in a relationship; being suppressed or exploited by people at home or work are negative and painful experiences for the mind.

If a child sees his parents - creating anxiety; fearing the future; having hurt and negative conversations; then he learns that particular way of being. These become his patterns of negativity as he grows up. If we have had negative patterns of thinking for a long-time - creating worry over small issues; anxiety about the future, not feeling worthy enough - then if there is an external crisis, it becomes a precipitating factor for us to have depression. Signs of low esteem are - getting hurt easily by other's behavior; feeling insulted; seeking approval and appreciation from others to feel good about the self.

Spiritual intake that we are a pure beautiful soul, child of God, loved and accepted by God unconditionally helps us to overcome depression. This new daily information creates new patterns of thinking. The old negative patterns of low self esteem get erased.

SUICIDE:

When one loses confidence in people around and future tends to commit suicide. Sudden failure, depression, or Guilt, disturbed thoughts lead to suicide. Ultimately when one feels that nobody is with him develop these tendencies. Sometimes monetary reasons may be there.

Suicide may be attempted, completed or accidentally completed. Those who are saved after attempt, suffer from loss of self esteem, guilt, pressure of family and friends. Spiritually, it is because one is not able to face people, family, extended family and friends. Young people are more vulnerable because mostly they are not able to share their grief and failure with their near and dear. They may not get proper support.

Suicide is a cry for help that ends in tragedy. An attempt, when the person feels that there is no hope in his future or people around him. It is an attempt to escape the constant emotional pain of helplessness and hopelessness. Reasons for suicide are - sudden professional or relationship failure; loneliness in old age; chronic illness or monetary reasons. In most cases there is a phrase of depression before attempting suicide. If a family accepts the mistakes of one another and is compassionate towards each other, then a person might not even think of suicide even if he has failed or made a very big mistake.

A soul on a journey carries the pain and Sanskars of the previous birth. Suicide can help a person to escape from the situation and people but will continue to carry the pain. Every problem has a solution. Spiritual groups can give us the power and support system.

BIPOLAR DISORDER:

When you have extreme moods of depression or excitement; spending more money or taking relation for granted; these extreme moods going on for some time with the interval of periods or so is bipolar disorder. Reasons whatsoever, may be, we must find out the ways to come out of that. People around should not think of reason but should find out the solution. It may be less of both types of moods then it is not bipolar. Instead of finding reason only we should consult somebody, whenever, anybody is suffering and is not well.

"Bipolar disorder is when our mind can go to two extreme poles for long periods of time. One pole is a state of depression, an attitude of hopelessness towards life and relationships. The second pole is pole of excitement of mania. For some people the phase of depression and phase of mania may come alternatively. Some may experience repeated episodes of depression and then episodes of mania. Few may experience only episodes of mania. If someone experiences either pole for more than two weeks, then they need treatment immediately.

Early intervention is extremely important, if there is only one episode and gets treated timely, it may never happen again. But if there are two or more episodes, then this possibility of it happening again will increase. One episode may last from 3 to 9 months.

SLEEP:

Early to bed, early to rise is a golden principle of life to remain healthy. Sleep should give you fresh energy. If you are not getting proper sleep, you may not feel that energetic body and mind. The reasons for poor quality of sleep can be- being extremely tired or very stressed or lack of physical activity or being overweight. The process of physical growth, removal of toxins, proper digestion and strength building of body happens smoothly during our sleep. Sleep processes our memories, emotions, excessive thoughts, overload of information and prepares us for the next day.

Good Sleep hygiene means - mentally packing up our thoughts by resolving issues of the day, gratitude for all the good that has happened, no worries about tomorrow, no planning for the next day, before sleeping. Conflicts before sleep, heavy meals or alcohol disturb our sleep quality.

Issues may not be resolved outside but resolve them inside before sleeping. Give the mind answer to the cause of anger, pain or hurt created and an understanding of other's behaviors and situations that happened during the day.

Addiction:

If we start using something for pleasure; use it repeatedly and then reach a stage where we feel we cannot live without it; feel restless when it is not there; we have reached a stage of psychological craving and withdrawals, then we are addicted.

Any behaviour which is having a negative impact on our life; which is not under our control; it is increasing and we are failing to stop it, is an addiction. Psychological addictions affect our day to day functioning, work life, relationships and sleep patterns.

Addiction can be to gambling, pornography, video games, technology, television, messaging, shopping, tea, coffee and also addiction to certain emotional patterns. Addiction does not finish by reducing it finishes only by stopping it completely.

Addiction is because the soul is searching for happiness and contentment outside. Addiction of anything reduces our will power, which we would need to face the challenges of life. Let us consciously keep ourselves away from gadgets and substances for couple of hours or days to increase our willpower.

Almost one third population of the country is using tobacco in one form or the other. Tobacco is not only as cigarette smoking, but chewing tobacco, tobacco as paste, or eaten in any other form is equally harmful for the health. Tobacco is the most highly addictive substance. For every 100 people who start having it, 90 people get addicted to it. In the past few year internationally men have started giving it up but women have started having it, adults are giving up but children are starting it.

Addiction of tobacco does not allow proper digestion of food; affects hormonal balance; reduces stamina, oxygenation of lungs and blood supply to the heart. A single cigarette has enough nicotine to cause death if it goes directly into the bloodstream. Tobacco is one of the only product known, which spoils our genetic material. It affects the healthy genes of the person and can be the cause of ill health or physical deformities in the next generation. Genetic problems can be controlled by our proper way of living. If we follow spiritual way of living and have positive thoughts we can avoid genetic problems.

Role of Spirituality:

Physical, mental, emotional, social health and spiritual health problems can be handled spiritually. But we can't do it just from taking thoughts as information. But when we will start using them in life, it will have effect on these illnesses. Infection needs to be treated with the help of medicine. When we are born then biologically from our parents and both sides of the family we get some genetic material. There is only a 30 percent chance of the genetic code affecting us, if we don't have a faulty life style and internal stress.

Physical health, mental health, social health and spiritual health are the four dimensions of our health. Spiritual health is the foundation for the other three dimensions. Spiritual means that our thoughts and actions are based on purity, peace, love power, truth and happiness, which are the original qualities of the soul.

Positive thinking is not about expecting the best to happen every time but accepting that whatever happens is the best for this moment. Visualizing the best to happen but then accepting the result and creating the right thoughts irrespective of what the outcome may be.

A meditative lifestyle will slow down our speed of thoughts, power of thoughts increases; heart rate reduces; blood pressure normalizes, sugar and cholesterol levels get regulated and patterns of the brain become positive.

We should spiritually understand that each soul is on a journey carrying different Sanskars, it will help us to accept people and situations and we will respond proactively.

Points to ponder

- It is a natural function of the body to remain healthy 80% of illness is because we are not using body properly. For remaining healthy and enjoying long life we have to use our body properly and take care of our eating habits.

- There are many diseases which are emotion related and are self created. The most powerful amongst them are Depression and Ego. They have to be treated by strengthening the soul through spirituality.

- The line between madness and sanity is very thin. Your emotional imbalance resulting in anger, jealousy, hatred, greed, etc may push you to cross the line from sanity to madness.

- A spiritual intake that we are pure beautiful soul, child of God, loved and accepted by God unconditionally helps us to overcome depression.

- When person feels that there is no hope in his future or people around him he tends to commit suicide. Spiritual Satsangs and meditation can give the power and support system to help us to come out of this suicidal tendency.

- Addiction is because the soul is searching for happiness and contentment outside. Spirituality teaches us we are happy and peaceful soul. It makes us understand that we have not to search happiness outside.

- Spiritual health is the foundation of our physical, mental, emotional and social health. Spiritual health means that our thoughts and actions are based on purity, peace, love, power, truth and happiness.

- A meditative lifestyle slows down the speed of thoughts so power of thoughts increases, heart rate reduces, blood pressure normalizes, sugar and cholesterol levels get regulated and patterns of brain become positive.